LIGHTS, CAMERA, MURDER

NIKKI HAVERSTOCK

COPYRIGHT

© 2016 by Ranch Dog Entertainment, LLC

ALSO BY NIKKI HAVERSTOCK

TARGET PRACTICE MYSTERIES
Death on the Range
Death at the Summit
Death at the Trade Show
Death Indoors
Death in the Casino
Death from Abroad

REALITY TV COZY MYSTERIES
Lights, Camera, Murder
Crossover Murder

For Linda, my beloved mother-in-law, who believes in me to
an embarrassing and almost delusional degree.

CHAPTER ONE

MELISSA

I wrote through lunch on a high-concept piece that used the sunset in a rural town as an allegory for old age. It was deep, it was meaningful, and it was total crap. I knew it even as I constructed beautiful sentence after beautiful sentence. The grammar was perfect, every comma in the correct place, and it was so pretentious I felt a bit nauseated. Or maybe that was the bloody Marys; one little glass had turned into three, and then it made sense to finish off the jug of tomato juice so I could throw away the evidence.

Thankfully, I was completely unaffected by the vodka. When the phone rang, I reached out to grab it and missed. "Oopsy." My voice was louder than expected. Maybe I was more affected than I thought. I managed to croak "Hello" into the receiver.

"Miss Melissa, this is Amanda from the front desk. Rebecca Sethi from *Sexy Socialites of Fishcreek Falls* is here to see you for a tour of the ranch as a possible filming location." The laughter in Amanda's voice was evident. She acted as our receptionist when we expected professional guests and played her role to the hilt. Amanda would run the hotel once it was built while my sister ran the resort and her husband ran the marketing of the resort. She and my sister had become inseparable since we moved here, and Amanda treated me like her favorite little sister, for which I was grateful.

"Be there in five" rushed out of my mouth as one long word before I slammed down the phone. I grabbed my cell phone off the desk in the corner of my bedroom and shoved it into my pocket. I slid the notebook into the bottom right drawer of my desk, the Drawer of Wayward Projects. It was difficult to close because of the weight of the notebooks filling the drawer. Each held a promising project that I had given up on. There were also countless thumb drives, DVDs, and CDs from the projects I had typed up. I was constantly switching up my writing methodology, hoping that I would eventually stumble on the key to success.

Not that I never finished any of those projects. I wrote articles relatively frequently. I had cowritten several memoirs for people with amazing stories and no desire or talent to write on their own: refugees, heroines, and women far more amazing than myself. That is how I had managed to spend ten years without anyone realizing I was a fraud.

I checked my laptop and found an email from my agent titled "New secret project available," and the first genuine thrill I'd experienced in months went through me. I ached to read it, but there wasn't time. Instead I locked my laptop so my family wouldn't see and ask.

I grabbed the half-sized bottle of vodka and slid it into an inside pocket in my winter jacket. The air was still too cool in the shade to go without outerwear. Didn't need vodka sitting around for everyone to see. I'd hide it later.

Once I was moving around the room, the mantle of

drunkenness fell away and instead left behind a light and airy coating of relaxation. It had been four hours with three lightweight drinks. I could handle this. Nothing scary. I could pretend to be a fully functioning adult that had her life together. I grabbed a washcloth from the bathroom and used the cold spring water to wipe around my eyes and neck. After touching up my makeup, I looked relaxed and smart. The illusion of having my life together was in place, though I could feel my fingertips straining to keep my act together.

I had moved here two years ago to focus on my writing. No excuses, just work. I had written hundreds of thousands of words, and each one brought me closer to the reality that I had nothing to say. If it wasn't for my few public and secret projects, I would have been convinced that I was incapable of finishing a book. Somewhere around the holidays this year, I'd stopped leaving the ranch. Around Valentine's Day, I'd stopped leaving the house. By Saint Patrick's Day, I'd stopped leaving my room except when my parents and my sister and her family moved out here. I thought that if I could just get quiet enough, cut out enough distractions, I would find some secret well of brilliance inside of me. So far, nothing.

I bounded out of my room and down the stairs toward the front door. Standing next to Amanda was a gal about my age who turned and smiled as I jogged down the stairs. She had dark, straight hair cut in an asymmetric bob that was longer in the front than the back. Instantly, I liked her. No idea why, but it was a welcome feeling.

She had a wide smile, and she extended a hand. "I'm Rebecca Sethi."

"Nice to meet you, Rebecca. I'm Melissa McBallister. I was under the impression that I was supposed to meet a—" I checked my hand, where I had taken notes in marker this morning "—Ryan Sethi, producer. Your husband?"

She waved a hand in front of her, dismissing the situation. "My brother. Unfortunately, he had a last-minute emergency. I offered to come out instead. I'm the director."

"I've always wondered about the difference between a producer and director."

"If this was a Hollywood movie or TV show or even an in-studio reality show, the differences would be many and exact, but on a small reality show like this, there's a ton of overlap. The easiest description is that as the director, I will be directing the activity where we are filming, while the producer will be setting things up ahead of time, afterwards, and off site."

I nodded along as though I understood then turned to Amanda. "Amanda, would you be willing to drive us around so I could sit in back with Rebecca and point things out?" The truth was that I didn't think it was wise to drive after drinking, no matter how little or long ago. Better safe than sorry.

"Absolutely, Meli, give me just a couple seconds." She left the entryway, and I turned back to Rebecca. "Tell me about this project."

She flipped open a leather portfolio and showed me a photo of five women. At the bottom in scrolling letters was the title, *Sexy Socialites of Fishcreek Falls*. Each woman was dressed in a tight-fitting dress and had one hand extended with a large glass snowflake balanced on her palm. The background was of the local ski slope, and fake snow covered that ground. "Here is a mockup of the title sequence, though the cast is not finalized."

"Have you considered a famous author?" said my sister, who had emerged from the hallway under the stairs.

I turned back to Rebecca. "Ignore my sister, Samantha. She thinks she's funny, but she's not."

Rebecca looked between Samantha and me before continuing. "*Sexy Socialites of Fishcreek Falls* will show the secret world of the rich and fabulous who live in one of the most beautiful ski towns on earth. Wait, are you a famous author?"

"Me? No, my mother is, I just play one on TV." Realizing who I was talking to, I corrected myself. "I mean, I don't play one on TV. I write, but... I'm not famous." I hitched my thumb over my shoulder at a wall full of large, framed pictures of my mother's book covers. "Our mom's famous."

Rebecca looked over my shoulder and let out a squeal. "Shut up! Your mom's Mary McBallister? Shut up, shut up. I love her."

I nodded; this was not a surprising reaction though a bit more intense than normal. "Yep, that's my mom."

"I can't believe it. I love her books, love them. I have read *Lost Widows* a million times." Suddenly her eyes grew to twice their size.

Amanda joined us with a bucket full of sodas and water. She had a gift for thinking of the perfect gracious touch that would make her an excellent host of the resort once it opened. "I grabbed some drinks. Are you ready?"

We stepped into the crisp spring air, then I crawled into the backseat of the ranch SUV, the vodka in the jacket across my lap knocking into my knee. Rebecca was still prattling on about the genius of my mother's books as Amanda slowly starting driving.

"...my senior thesis on her work. In fact, I even got a tattoo in honor of finishing the project. Oh, and her recent work is just as..."

She was so excited and moved. Eventually she would want to know about my work, and the pale comparison would be impossible to deny. The extent to which I fell short would be breath-taking. My throat tightened as a panic attack welled up in my chest. It was hard to breathe even though I was gulping in air in staccato gasps.

The car lurched to a stop, and Amanda turned around in her seat. "Mel, are you okay?"

"I need air." I threw open the door and leaped to my escape. I caught my arm in the seat belt on the way out and flipped around before landing hard on my hands and knees in the mud. The thick brown liquid squished up through my fingers and seeped through my jeans.

Darting off the ground, I ran for a small patch of trees, where spring snow still clung in the deep shadows of the aspens and pines. Spring was slow to arrive in the high elevations of the Rocky Mountains.

I paused by a small cluster of flowers pushing up through the snow, their leaves a new green. Briefly, I appreciated the beauty of the droplets of liquid catching the light on the petals before I vomited bloody Marys all over them. The thick tomato juice dripped off a leaf from the one remaining flower that still stood upright. The rest of the bouquet was pressed to the ground, hidden beneath a tsunami of mixed drinks. I didn't remember the mimosa, but I'd obviously had one as well. I pushed off the tree I had leaned against and jogged away from the mess toward another knot of trees.

I pressed my hands together to alleviate the sting from falling. The cool air helped clear my thoughts. I was being silly and overreacting, but there was no way to undo my dramatic car escape except to continue. Maybe I could run away and live in the woods like Jack London's dog in *Call of the Wild*. But then where would I get more vodka?

I disappeared into the patch of woods and slipped behind a large aspen. I braced my hands on my knees as a tear slipped down my cheek. My ribs on one side hurt from the vodka bottle smacking me as I had run. I pulled it out and took a sip, coughing hard as the alcohol stripped my mouth of moisture. If I was going to have a nervous break-down in the woods, then I was going to go full bore. I guzzled more vodka.

I heard running feet approach then Rebecca calling to me. "Are you okay? Did I upset you?"

"No," I shook my head then couldn't bear to lie anymore. "Yes, you did, but it's not your fault. Do you know she was twenty-nine when *Lost Widows* was published? That's one year older than me."

I gestured to my chest, forgetting about the vodka. The hard glass smacked my sternum and drove the air from my lungs with a wheeze. "I had the best education, the best upbringing, every advantage in life, and yet I am so far behind that I can never catch up. What excuse do I have?"

I gestured wildly and smacked a branch overhead. Drops of water rained down on me as my voice rose. "None, not a one! I'm a failure. Do you know what it's like to know that despite every advantage in life, you're utterly useless?"

My voice wobbled at the end of my diatribe, and I gulped in big, dramatic snorts of air, eyes watering. I couldn't even bear to look at her. I didn't know this woman at all, and yet I was bare before her. The silence stretched out, and I began to pray that she would leave me to my shame.

"Family can do that to you. My mother won an Oscar for her documentaries on refugees and was recently decorated as one of the most important women filmmakers of her generation, and I'm working on a reality show about sexy socialites." She waited until I caught her eye then smiled. "I've been working like a dog for weeks. How about we just sit for a bit and chat?"

Amanda had followed Rebecca down but had stopped a dozen feet away.

I looked at her, sniffling and wiping my sleeve across my nose. "Amanda, I'm just going to stay here for a bit."

Amanda would keep the whole thing quiet and give me some space. She was great like that and proved it by smiling and leaving.

Rebecca took a swig from her soda and sat on the fallen tree. The log shifted and spun, knocking her over backwards. She landed flat on her back with her legs up in the air. I raced over and offered her a hand while we giggled and righted the log. We twisted it until it sat firmly then both took a seat at opposite ends.

Why would a director on the verge of filming a reality TV show sit in the woods with me? If this were a book or movie, she could be the wise and kind stranger that provided me with the perfect information at the perfect time to change the course of my life forever.

I eyed her, and she didn't look anything like Yoda. I probably wasn't destined to be a Jedi. More likely Cinderella. I squinted. She had nice round cheeks and looked like she knew her way around a wand.

What advice could she give me? The perfect plot to my book could work. Or she was here to tell me that I was a witch or the heir to a throne in a far-away country. Those were also good ideas. Which would be more interesting: endless power or true love and riches?

"You look really intense," she said. "What's going on inside your head?"

My thoughts shattered into a million directions. "I'm sorry. I was... thinking." My family was used to me disappearing into my head, but I tried to control it in public.

"About?" Her tone wasn't judgy and seemed genuinely interested.

"I was just making up stories in my head, imagining the reasons you would be sitting with me out here. I like to entertain myself by trying to guess what people are like." I avoided her eyes, embarrassed. Daydreaming was something I'd always been embarrassed by.

"Because you're a writer. That makes sense. What kind of things do you observe? And what do you think about me?" She looked at me with curiosity lighting up her eyes.

Rather than get into my original idea, I focused on her. "Well, you're cute and adaptable. You didn't freak out when I leaped from the car, so I think you are used to adventure and into high drama."

She smiled and laughed, nodding at me to continue.

"Let's see. What else? You work with your brother, and your mother was also in film, so I'm guessing you are close to your family. Is your brother older or younger? On this project, is he your boss, employee, or peer?"

"He's older and my boss." She rested her elbow on her knee and leaned her chin on her palm.

"And your dad? Any other siblings?"

"Only the two of us. Dad died when I was nine. He and Mom were filming about child soldiers, and he was shot when they were ambushed right as they finished production. "

I pulled back. "I'm so sorry."

She gave a weak smile. She had probably heard that a

million times. "It was very important work. It brought a huge issue to the world's awareness."

I nodded. If the dad had been a risk taker, then... "Who is more cautious, you or your brother?"

"Ryan, for sure."

My thoughts swirled in my head. "So you've always been protected, first by your father then your older brother. You can take risks because your brother has your back. He makes sure you have work. You both are passionate about your jobs because you followed in your family's career path, but I'm guessing he goes the safer route, while you make bigger gambles because you have family to save you. It would be a great story, with the TV show being your biggest triumph."

I was pleased by my analysis until I noticed the smile had left her face.

"Oh, Rebecca, I'm sorry. I got excited and didn't think about—"

She cut me off. "No, no, you're fine. You have some good observations that I hadn't thought of before."

"I really am sorry. I didn't want to talk about my family either. I shouldn't have brought it up."

"No more family talk. Do you want to tell me about this ranch, or is that off the table as well?"

I twisted on the log to face Rebecca. "This ranch"—I gestured toward the large house—"has been our vacation home since I was a kid, and a couple of years ago I moved up here to work on my writing. Over there is the new ranch that is much bigger that my parents and older sister are converting into a dude ranch slash fishing mecca slash hunting lodge extraordinaire. We bought it last year." I pointed to the barely visible hive of activity a few miles down the road.

"I saw a sign on the way here. Anything finished?"

"Nope. They just started construction a few weeks ago when the ground was ready. My family moved in here full time last month. Can you believe that I am twenty-eight and living with not only my parents but my sister and her family as well? I really need to move out. But the construction site would be a great place for you to film your reality show. Instead of throwing wine and flipping tables, the socialites can use nail guns and two-by-fours. Really take the reality drama to a new level."

She chuckled. "The ratings would be amazing."

Amanda returned from the car with the bucket of drinks. "I'll just leave these here." She set the bucket on the ground and gave my shoulder a squeeze before walking back to the car, getting in and taking a U-turn toward the house.

I grabbed a glass from the bucket and poured a generous helping of vodka then added some citrus soda before starting a second glass for Rebecca.

"No vodka for me. I still need to drive back in about an hour."

I held my glass aloft to her soda can. "Glad you could join me for my mental health crisis in the woods. Cheers."

"No place I'd rather be. Cheers." She clicked her can against my glass, and we sipped in silence.

RYAN

"Ryan." Stacey Rickman's husband kept using my name. He had probably heard that using people's first name repeatedly made them more likely to give into your requests, but all it was doing was irritating me. "If you want my wife to appear in your show, you'll need to figure out a way to make it possible. I want to be able to approve the episodes before they air. Stacey, quit doing that." The last line he snapped at his wife, who was tugging on his sleeve.

I took a deep breath; this conversation had been forty-five minutes of verbal circles. "That will not be possible. I'm sorry we couldn't get this worked out, but you'll have to excuse me. I need to get back to my production meeting."

There wasn't any point in arguing any longer. I couldn't accommodate Rickman's request, and I was done. I flipped shut the leather portfolio holding my notepad and Stacey's unsigned cast contract.

"When you change your mind, give us a call." Mike Rickman beamed. He was the world's worst negotiator, having talked his way right out of his wife's contract through needless demands. I wouldn't even see the episodes before they aired, yet he expected to get approval rights? Ridiculous.

I held the door open for them, and as they left, my phone rang. Recognizing the number, I answered and didn't bother with formalities. "Hey Ian, bad news, we lost Stacey Rickman. I'll have to replace her ASAP if we are still going to start filming soon, and—"

"Easy, Ryan, you'll replace her no problem. I have faith in you." Ian's gravelly voice came through the line, relaxed and calm. That was more than enough reason for me to be suspicious.

"Why aren't you freaking out? What's wrong?" I had worked with Ian enough to know that his calm attitude was a lie. Might as well get the bad news out of the way now.

"Remember that show I was pitching to the networks? A bunch of reality stars will pair up and compete in a dance competition. The network bought it, and that's great news for you."

I had a sinking feeling. Ian was never an optimist. "Great news for me?"

"Yes, *Sexy Socialites* is all yours. I spoke to the network and assured them of your brilliance, and they are willing to have your production company take the lead. Bobby, the data wrangler, is still flying over tomorrow. He'll fly the footage back every Thursday to my editing studio, but I already cancelled my flight. I need to stay in L.A. for preproduction."

I held my breath while I weighed my reply, but that wasn't good enough for Ian.

"You know, Ryan, there are a lot of people that would kill for this opportunity. In fact, if you aren't—"

"Ian, I'm very thankful for the opportunity. I was just deep in thought about all the things I need to handle. This is very exciting." I knew my voice was not conveying genuine enthusiasm, but hopefully it was good enough.

"Excellent. I'll have my assistant email over the new contracts from the network and a few documents that I was planning on going over when I arrived. Oh, one more small thing. They've cut the season to four episodes from eight."

"That's a *big* thing."

"They were never super sold on the idea of the show to begin with, and they got some pitch about upscale trailer park realtors. If this show takes off, they might consider going back to eight episodes, but if not... most of these shows only last a season anyways. I have to go. Be in touch."

I rubbed the back of my neck. Becca was going to be devastated to hear our season had been cut in half. This was her directorial debut, and she was also convinced it would be her big break. But with only four episodes, we were doomed from the start.

CHAPTER TWO

Melissa

Becca checked her phone after it beeped then slid it into her jacket pocket. We'd been making idle chitchat while sipping our drinks. The acidic tang of my drink stripped away that leftover taste of tomato in my mouth and throat. Usually vomiting is a sign that you should stop drinking, but I was no quitter.

"I don't normally leap from moving vehicles and race off into the woods."

Rebecca waved a hand and winked at me. "Who *hasn't* done that? I appreciate someone honest about what they are feeling. So many people have this mask on and spend energy pretending to be fine and normal. The world doesn't need more normal. That's why people love reality television."

"Oh?"

"Yes. The best reality shows are made of people that are authentic. They act and react in a real way. People are envious of that, the ability to really say what they are thinking and doing what they really want to do. I've worked on several shows..." She looked down at her drink, opening her mouth to speak a few times.

"What's the show about? *Sexy Socialites of Fishcreek Falls*, I mean."

"We'll have five local ladies in their late twenties through early forties. They're rich or prestigious or both, and we follow them in their daily life, interacting."

I pursed my lips. "That doesn't sound very interesting. What am I missing?"

She tilted her head to the side. "What do you mean? It's a very typical setup for these types of shows."

I leaned forward, and the bubbles in my drink fizzed to the surface and hissed. The lemon and lime scent cleared my head and tickled my nose. "I've never seen that kind of reality show. I mean, I've seen a couple of competition shows like the one with fashion design or that baking show from Britain, but that's it."

Her mouth hung open. "Seriously? There's a million of those shows."

"I know." I shook my head. "I haven't had a television set since high school. I watch some things on the Internet, but mostly I read."

She gaped at me as if I had fallen from outer space, looking me up and down. Given how awkward and clumsy I had been since we met, it did seem like it was my first time dealing with Earth's gravity.

"You're a writer," she said. "So I guess that makes sense."

I swirled my drink around. The vodka was clear in the soda, but it created lines of movement as I tipped the glass left and right. I listed too hard in the process and threw a hand onto the log to catch myself before I tipped over.

"What do you write about? Is it like your mom's stuff?"

I groaned before I could catch myself. I downed my drink then poured myself more. Sucking air through my teeth, I cleared my mouth of vodka. "I've helped cowrite some memoirs, about a half dozen since high school. You might have seen some of them."

"Like a ghostwriter?"

"Not exactly. My name is on the cover either as a coauthor or 'as told to.' It isn't a secret." At least those weren't.

"So nonfiction. Cool."

I hesitated. "I also write fiction, but I'm not published in that... Can we not talk about my writing... it's... I mean, I don't want to be rude but... it's not going so well and..." I poured the rest of the vodka into my glass.

She waved her hands. "I totally understand." She grabbed a soda from the bucket and tossed it over. "I want to ask you something. It's a favor, but I want you to listen all the way through before you react."

"Sure." I took a long drink from my glass.

"One of our cast members dropped out, and I think you should take her spot."

I gasped in surprise and inhaled a mouthful of soda and vodka. Spitting out what I could, I collapsed over my knees to cough the liquid out of my lungs.

Rebecca pounded on my back as I coughed. "Oh no, don't throw up again. I don't think I could—" She gagged a few times.

"I'm fine." I wiped the drool off my chin and breathed out before taking a small sip of my drink. "Are you okay?" I transferred my drink to my far hand to hold out to the side so I could rub her back with my close hand.

She was still gagging and started making small "erurp" noises then swallowed hard. Her eyes watered and her face was red. "Sorry, I just—" She covered her mouth and bent over. She held up her index finger then stood up. "Sorry, we all have our weaknesses, and mine is..." Her face went pale.

I guided her back to where she had been sitting.

"I'm fine. Will you consider doing the show?" Her eyes were red and watery. Tears streamed down her face from the gagging, and she wiped them away.

I blew out my breath, sat back down, and took a sip as a stall tactic. I didn't have much of an opinion about being on television. It couldn't be that hard, but why would I want to? "I'm a writer."

"Think of the exposure you will get."

"I guess. But my own projects aren't out yet. I could use exposure for them, if I ever get something finished." I hadn't meant to share the last bit, but it slipped out without thinking.

"But think of the creativity fodder you would get from the experience. I write too, mostly screenplays, and when I get stuck in a funk, the best thing I can do is go on a grand adventure. Within a few weeks, I have more ideas than I can handle."

That was encouraging news. "Really?" Perhaps this was what I needed. I would walk through fire if it would help my writing. "How much time would it take?"

"Not much at all. Basically Sunday evening when the show airs until Wednesday evening for two months. Not that entire time, but I know there would be basically nothing going on Thursday to Sunday."

"But it wouldn't air until much later, right? So for filming it would be Monday through Wednesday. That would leave tons of time to write." I contemplated the facts.

"So much time to write, absolutely, but it's going to air the Sunday after we film. That was the big hook in our pitch to that network. Usually there is a big delay where friendships are made and broken several times over. With social media, the initial impact of the drama is lost. With the episodes airing right after the filming, we keep the fresh 'just happening' vibe." She made little finger quotes as she spoke. Her voice got louder and faster as she talked.

"Uh, sure, doesn't matter so long as I have time to work. You really think this will help my writing?"

"Totally. Absolutely." She let out a high-pitched giggle. "I'll just call my brother, and he can come meet you. He has final approval. He'll love you."

She hopped and skipped out to the road and was on the phone within seconds. Pacing back and forth, she gestured wildly with her free hand.

A feeling of unease crawled up my back. Why had I said yes? I took another sip of my drink. I hadn't watched any of the shows she described, but I knew plenty about them from various news stories and research. The media reported on reality stars in a manner normally reserved for movie stars or politicians. I often heard of their wild escapades, but those must have been rare instances. It would be over in no time. Then I could use all my experiences for my writing. What was the worst that could happen?

I gathered up the glasses and empty cans and stuck them in the bucket and joined Rebecca on the road.

RYAN

I put down my phone and pushed the rejected applications for *Sexy Socialites* across the table. "Beth, will you get me a second set of directions to that ranch out of town? I gave mine to Becca."

"I can print out another copy. What's up?" Beth pressed a few buttons on her laptop.

"Becca thinks one of the gals at the ranch would make an awesome socialite for the show, and it's the best lead we have so far." I tossed my messenger bag over my head.

Beth got up to grab some papers from the printer. "Here you go."

"Can you go with me? I know you have a lot of work to do, but you could be my navigator, maybe look at some stuff on your phone about her on the way over and give me your general impression. If she could work, I'd want to finalize it tonight."

"No problem, you're the boss." She gathered up her tablet and purse. She was the most organized person I'd ever worked with.

We headed out to the parking lot outside the hotel. We had been loaned a floor of the hotel in exchange for some on-air promotion. It was mud season, the two times a year between winter snow season and summer. Spring and fall were the lull between the two tourist seasons when most hotels sat empty. I unlocked the rental vehicle. "Do you have the list finalized for the locations we've secured and related promotion?"

"Yes, two days ago. I emailed you a copy and uploaded a backup copy to the production cloud server. Head toward the far side of town like we're going to the airport, then we'll go north out where all the ranches are."

"Can you look up Melissa McBallister and see what you can find?" The traffic was a mix of dinged-up ranch and work trucks, high-end sedans, and SUVs, but all of them were muddy. The town sat in a valley at the base of the ski slopes. Through the town ran a river, while the majority of the houses clung to the hillsides. It took us no more than ten minutes to drive the length of town even hitting every red light.

"There's a ton on her and her family, assuming this is really her. Are her parents Mary and Bob McBallister?"

"I think so. Her mom is definitely Mary McBallister. She wrote *Lost Widows*. I didn't make the connection when I sent Becca out there, but she told me all about it when she called."

Beth let out a whistle. "Impressive. I read that in a college lit class along with some of her other stories. Bob's no slouch either. According to this article, he sold his company a few years ago for an undisclosed amount, but 'experts estimate it would be near the billion-dollar mark.'"

"What kind of company?"

"It was an ebook company, the kind where people can publish their own books. It was bought out by a bigger company. Take the next right at the light."

I turned right. The road weaved between some hills then crested another. The city was no longer visible in the rearview mirror, and stretched out ahead were open fields of new green and tree-covered mountains in the distance.

"It's gorgeous out here." Beth pressed her face up against the window. "Reception is getting worse. If you have any more questions, you better ask them quick."

"Anything weird come up on the search?"

"Not really. Let me see this article on the family. Three kids, all were investors in the publishing business. Nice. They probably got a pretty penny from that deal. Internet's gone. Turn left at that dirt road."

The dirt road veered off to the left toward a mountain. There was a ranch on either side of the corner but no street name. "Are you sure?"

"Have I ever led you astray? Yes, turn here. It's back

behind that mountain, down this county road. Oh, the article has a picture at the end. She's cute as a button. She has a pretty well-known family, money from the sounds of it, and she's interested in doing it. Even if she has the personality of a tree stump, she might work."

"I would prefer something better than 'might work,'" I grumbled. We bounced and jostled down the rough road. Occasionally the road dipped, and I carefully maneuvered the car around the deepest puddles, but mud splashed up the windows when I spun the tires on one side.

Beth rolled her eyes at me. "Let's problem solve this. Is there anyone you know of that would be better?"

"No, unless you saw someone?"

"We were looking at the same list, and no. Can we go with the existing four cast members?"

"Not really. We could, but four is not a great number because it is so easy to split into two and two for a fight. An odd number is great because there is always a tiebreaker or a loose cannon that someone is trying to get onto their side of an argument. If you get much more than five, it is tough for the audience to get to know any of them, but if there are too few, then there isn't enough personality to carry a show. I think five is the perfect number. That reminds me of some advice I got. Melissa needs a social tie to someone on the cast."

When I had gotten the job on *Sexy Socialites*, I'd called a few friends for advice on casting the show, and a few key pieces had emerged from multiple sources. "That's how we got the initial applications. They said it is important that everyone has some existing tie to another cast member. We should have brought the cast photos."

"And maybe a blank contract and a freshly revised schedule for four weeks of shooting?" She pulled out a stack of papers and wagged them at me with a smug smile. "Take a left."

I veered left down another unmarked dirt road, which was even rougher than the last, a feat I hadn't thought possible. "You're a lifesaver."

"I know. Stick with me and you'll be at the top in no time."

I turned onto a narrower road that cut through a thicket of trees and over a bridge. The river below must feed into the river that ran through town. "I'll be happy when I go back to filming commercials. Nice, safe, manageable TV commercials. Is this the right place?" I could see a nice but plain house with young children playing in front.

A man with a cowboy hat approached the car, a gun visible on his hip. He had an ample brown mustache above the thin line of his mouth. "Can I help you?"

"I'm Ryan Sethi. I'm supposed to meet my sister Rebecca Sethi, who had a—"

He cut me off. "I met her earlier. You can go on up to the house." He pointed to where the road continued around a corner.

I rolled up the window. "It's the real Wild West around here."

Beth was beaming. "I dig it. This place would really drive the 'home of the wild and rich' frontier theme. Perfection."

We rounded a stand of trees and emerged before a gorgeous and immense log cabin. I wondered if I should still call it a log cabin when it must have been well over ten thousand square feet. It was as lovely as any of the houses in town, but the way it was perched on an outcrop overlooking miles of open land, it seemed more impressive.

Rebecca bounded out the front door, and trailing

behind her was a blonde woman. Her hair was all shades of blonde, flipping one way and the other, a little curl twisting under her chin. She was curvy, with a bounce in her step that drew my eyes. "I want her..." I swallowed. "For the show."

Beth snorted. "Sure, that's what you meant."

MELISSA

I was sitting with Rebecca in the kitchen, pounding water and hoping that I could get rid of the acidic taste at the back of my throat when she hopped up.

She ran to the window to peer out then turned around to tell me, "Ryan's here."

I followed her out to the front door. Amanda popped her head out of her office as we passed. "You're back. Did you finish the tour yet? Who just drove up?"

"Don't worry about it," I said over a shoulder then closed the front door behind me. The issue of telling everyone what I had agreed to wasn't a bridge I wanted to cross just yet.

Standing next to the car was a shorter, brown-haired gal clutching a tablet to her chest, a backpack thrown over one shoulder. On the opposite side of the car was Ryan. Tall, dark, and handsome was a clichéd and perfect description. He approached with an unreadable expression and the fluid grace of an athlete. His broad shoulders filled out his shirt, which pulled across a muscular chest. Even in the cool weather, he wore short sleeves, showing off strong arms, and his long, lean legs ate up the distance between us in easy strides. Why didn't I meet guys like this when I needed a date?

I suddenly felt shy and uneasy in my skin. Did I need to impress him, or was he trying to impress me? What in the world made a good reality star?

"Welcome. Why don't you guys come in. It's getting cold." I stepped back to the door. The sun had dipped behind the mountains even though sunset wasn't for a while. The air had gone from chilly to flat-out cold.

As Ryan approached, I extended a hand. He had a firm handshake, the kind my dad said you could trust a man or woman by.

Rebecca excitedly introduced everyone. "Ryan, this is Melissa. Melissa, this is my brother Ryan, also known as the producer of *Sexy Socialites of Fishcreek Falls*. And this is Beth. I wasn't expecting you to tag along."

Beth extended her hand. "I'm the one that keeps this ship on course. This is a beautiful home."

I smiled back at her. "It's the family vacation home. Wait, was. It's not a vacation home anymore." I laughed. I didn't really need to get into the whole living arrangement. I opened the door to discover my sister Samantha and both my parents standing there. Waiting. "Hey, guys."

Becca, Beth, and Ryan filed in after me, and I repeated the introductions. As everyone shook hands, my mother gave me a look and raised her eyebrows before turning to Ryan. "So nice to have you here."

I hadn't intended to tell my family my plan to go on the reality show just yet, so I didn't want to volunteer why Ryan and Beth were here. Perhaps my relatives would just leave on their own.

Sam, my sister with the worst timing ever, turned to Becca. "Does this mean you'll be filming here for your show?"

Becca looked at me. "Um, maybe?"

Sam scrunched up her eyebrows. "Oh, I just assumed because your brother drove out here..." She looked between the *Sexy Socialites* production staff and me. "What's going on?"

"Uh..." Could I lie? That wasn't how I had been raised. I blew out a sigh. "They've asked me to consider being on the show"

"Really? That's awesome." Sam beamed and rubbed her hands together, chortling.

My mother placed a hand on her chest. "My daughter? On reality TV? Having the resort on the show is one thing. That's advertising, a commodity, but my daughter's not for sale."

Rebecca stepped forward. "She won't be for sale. *Sexy Socialites of Fishcreek Falls* is a show about—"

My father's face was bright red. "*Sexy Socialites*? Sexy? No one told me that. What kind of smut show is this? No daughter of mine will be on a show with the word 'sexy' in the title!" he bellowed.

Next to me, Beth whispered under her breath. "Oh boy."

"Dad, Dad, it's okay," I pleaded. "It's just a title to make it sound interesting. Right, Ryan?"

The entire room swung around to stare at Ryan. Dad clenched a fist.

"Smut?" Ryan took a half step forward as his voice echoed in the entryway.

"Not smut." Rebecca grabbed Ryan's arm. "There won't be anything scandalous like pole dancing."

My mother gasped. "I should hope not. Oh dear. We have a reputation to uphold. What will people think? 'Sexy,' that's just so tacky." She covered her mouth, her face pale, and collapsed into a convenient chair.

Ryan took another step toward the door. "This was a bad idea. We can show ourselves out."

"Wait." Samantha held out a hand. "Please give us a few minutes. Amanda, why don't you show Ryan, Rebecca, and Beth to the dining room?"

Once the door clicked shut behind them, the tears started flowing. "How could you embarrass me like that?" My lip was wavering as I covered my mouth. The fumes of liquor from my breath tickled my nose. Why does family push my buttons so much? I really needed a blender. A situation like this deserved frozen margaritas.

My mother narrowed her eyes at me and hissed out her reply between clenched teeth, "Don't you use that tone with me. I *am* your mother."

My father put a hand on my shoulder as I gulped back a sob. "Okay, okay, settle down."

Sam looked between my parents and me. "Mom, Dad, I think Melissa should do this. Let me explain." The last bit raced out as Dad's jaw dropped.

Sam never backed me up. She was the oldest and took the job of bossing me around and being superior very seriously.

"I checked out a few of the other shows on the station and the pitch package of this show. The cast will be having lunches, dinners, doing some charity work. It's only an eight-week season. I've seen these types of shows, and really, they're nothing like what you're thinking."

My mother took her angry, beady eyes off me and swiveled to Sam. "You watch these kind of shows? Oh, Sami."

"They're not like that, Mom. They're a little like those soaps you used to watch."

My mother had been addicted to daytime soap operas

when we were kids. They had been her guilty pleasure. Every day, even when she was on deadline, it was her time. That had been drilled into our heads.

At the memory, Mom flushed a little and looked away. The moment seemed less tense than it had been.

I softened my tone as much as possible. "Mom, Dad, it will only be a few weeks, and I doubt anyone will even watch. I mean, come on, who wants to watch me on TV?" I hiccupped then grimaced at the taste in my mouth. I really needed a breath mint.

"Oh, honey, don't say that." My mother shook her head.

"I just mean, it won't 'ruin the family reputation.' I just think the adventure would be good for me. I'm struggling with my writing, and a year of cutting out everything hasn't helped. Maybe I need to get out. Live a little. I really don't want this to be a big deal." It was more than a little embarrassing that I was twenty-eight and practically begging my parents to let me do something. It might be time to research therapy. "I don't need your permission, but I'd like your support."

Dad blew out a breath and nodded at my mother.

She sighed. "You're an adult. You can make your own decisions."

It was hardly a rallying cry of support, but I would take it. "Thank you."

My sister squeezed my arm. "I'll go negotiate with you. Then we can send over the contract to James."

James was the middle child and an entertainment lawyer.

I nodded. "Thanks, Sis." I turned to my parents, and I knew they were disappointed, and it twisted my stomach. "I love you guys. It'll be okay." I hugged each of them. I wasn't even sure if I wanted to do the show anymore, but that should be my decision.

My parents headed toward the kitchen. The second they rounded the corner in the hall, Sam pulled me in close by my arm and hissed into my ear. "Do *not* screw this up. My butt's on the line now too, so if you embarrass me, so help me..."

I jerked my arm out of her grasp and rubbed it. "Holy hand grenades, you're trying to tear my arm off. I thought you were on my side."

"I am... kinda. I called some friends, and if we can get the resort onto the show, I can get coverage. You being on the show will get us so many articles and features. I want to start booking clients for next winter, and the exposure we'll get from you being on the show..." She rubbed her hands together and squealed. "This weekend we'll drive over to Denver and get you a whole new wardrobe, and we can get your hair cut. Oh, we can get the resort name put on your jacket right here." She poked a fingernail into my left breast.

"Watch it." I rubbed my chest. "So you *do* think this is a good idea? I'm getting some mixed signals here."

She shrugged. "It's worth the gamble. Of course, I'm not the one gambling; if you end up being a hot mess, I'll disinherit you. Now let's get the resort on TV."

CHAPTER THREE

RYAN

Amanda directed us down to a large room with a bank of windows that looked out to the valley. The view didn't offset my frustration with the whole situation. I was wasting an evening of time we needed to be working. I was most angry at Melissa. She must have known her parents would disagree.

When a phone rang, Amanda left to answer it and carefully closed the door behind her.

Becca got up and raced to the door, pressing her ear to the edge. Voices rose and fell in the entryway of the home.

I turned to Beth. "I guess that answers that question. We should have left."

"Are you kidding? This family is totally all up in each other's grill. I love it! The way the mother swooned at the thought of her daughter doing something tacky. We have to get her on the show and film here. Maybe we could get footage of her fainting."

"It's not healthy. This family is codependent." And rich and beautiful. Or at least Melissa was.

Beth rolled her eyes at me. "Like you're one to talk. Besides, emotionally healthy people don't make for good TV."

Becca turned away from the door and shushed us. "I want to hear what they're saying."

Beth pulled out a contract and started filling it in with Melissa's name.

Becca fist pumped the air and scooted back to join us. "I think she's in." She gave a high five to Beth and sat down.

I pulled out a chair at the head of the table, next to Beth. "I don't know. She seems sweet. Maybe this isn't the right kind of project for her."

Becca leaned forward to see around Beth. "Are you kidding? She's perfect, and we need another cast member. We'll get her to sign, then we can finalize the schedule for the next eight weeks."

I winced. "About that... the network is cutting the season to four weeks for now. They're still open to a full season if we get the ratings."

She paled. "How could we get any ratings? It'll take that amount of time to even get people to start watching, let alone for the show to catch on. We can't make the show work in four weeks."

"I'm sorry, Sis. I don't have any control over it."

Her eyes were shiny and red. A tear spilled out. "But..."

It twisted my gut to see her cry. "It'll be okay. There'll be lots more shows. I promise."

The door opened, and Becca wiped the tears away as Samantha and Melissa entered and sat opposite Beth and Becca.

Samantha cleared her throat. "Sorry about that, but we've got it all settled now. Do you have a copy of the contract? I want to send it to our lawyer to review."

Beth hesitated but held up the contract. "It's right here, but we really need to finalize the cast ASAP."

Samantha smirked. "Don't worry. He'll do it quickly." She extended a hand for the contract then took pictures of it with her phone. "I'll be right back." She exited the room.

"Melissa, can I talk to you?" I stood up, and when she nodded, I walked over to the windows. She was so pretty and sweet, it wouldn't be right to let her join the cast without knowing the risks.

She looked up at me with her green eyes, curls of blonde hair falling across an eye until she pulled it behind an ear. "Yes?"

"I want to make sure that you have really thought about this. Reality TV will put you in front of a large, judgmental audience—"

"You think I don't know that? I may not watch it, but I live on planet Earth." She crossed her arms, pushing her breasts together.

I tried to be a gentleman but, being a human, couldn't stop my eyes from dipping down at the movement. I swallowed hard and tore my eyes back to her face. "I don't know if this project is the best—"

She gasped. "I can't believe this! You don't want me on the show. You jerk! I got into a huge fight with my family over this." She narrowed her eyes at me, and I saw the resemblance to her mother.

I took a step back. Why couldn't she tell that I was looking out for her breast—*best*, I was looking out for her best interests? "No, no, that's not what I meant. We still want you on the show, but maybe you shouldn't do it. Is this really what you want to do?"

She stepped toward me and aggressively jabbed a finger toward my chest. "You're not my mom. You can't tell me what to do. Wait, I'm an adult. My mom can't tell me what to do, either. Where's Sam? Where's that contract? I'm taking care of this right now."

A door creaked, and Samantha was on the phone with the contract in her hand. Melissa stormed off toward her and snatched the contract from her. "What did James say?"

Becca glared at me. "What are you doing?" she hissed at me.

Samantha looked around the room before turning back to Melissa. "He did a quick once over and said it was pretty standard, but he wants to send over some minor notes tonight for the production company's review. He's confident the contract will work, but he does want to talk to you, in private, when you get a chance."

Melissa had zoned out at some point to read over the contract. She flipped through the pages quickly. "No. Tell him it's fine." She carried the contract over to Beth. "May I?" She gestured toward the pen. "Let's get this all finished up. Samantha, we can head down to Denver and buy me some boots. After today, I need and deserve some kick-butt boots. Lots of them." She flipped through and signed on all the dotted lines. "There. Do you want me or not?"

She was awful mouthy. I ground my teeth before replying. "Yes, fine, whatever." I signed the contract. "Beth, can you give her the schedule and ride back with Rebecca? I have things I need to do." Like get away from spoiled women. I had a hand on the door to the dining room before I realized that I couldn't storm off. "I will see you next Monday, Melissa. Good bye."

By the time I got into the car, I had cooled off. I was in charge of this whole production, and I shouldn't have let anyone get under my skin, especially a cast member. Staying above the fray was a quality that I prided myself on having. Never let the talent see what you think of them. She wasn't prepared for the invasion of privacy that was to come. If she wanted to go on TV and potentially ruin her life—viewers would hate her for being rich and gorgeous—then it was none of my business.

MELISSA

My heart twisted a little in my chest when Ryan left the dining room. He was arrogant and had no right to suggest what was best for me, but the room seemed less exciting with him gone.

Sam checked her watch. "If we're going to Denver, then I need to make arrangements with Stan." Stan was her husband, a marketing expert, and they had two small children. Perhaps this Denver shopping trip was more about some quiet time than helping me.

I turned to Rebecca and Beth. "So, what now?"

A noise in the driveway pulled my attention to the window. Ryan drove by. His profile was striking with his commanding nose.

"Don't mind Ryan," Rebecca said. "He can be an old sourpuss, but he's a great producer."

Beth snorted then pulled out some files from a folder. "Fill out this form for me. I need all your contact information so I can get ahold of you. Tonight, I will send over a packet of information. I'll be your contact person for everything, if you are running late for filming, if you are lost, if you forget something, anything. Me. Everyone else on set has a job. My job is to coordinate everything."

I nodded and filled out the form then slid it back across the table.

"Here." She slid me another form. "Enter all this into your phone, and can you send me a note from your primary email?" It had her contact information.

"Got it." I pulled out my phone and typed in the information while she sorted through papers. "Cell reception is really sketchy here, so I put down my home number as well."

She laid out four headshots. "These will be your cast-mates. Do you know any of them?"

The pictures were of beautiful women. "A few of them look vaguely familiar. This one right here"—I pointed at the picture on the far left—"could she go to my dermatologist's office?"

"Yes, she's married to the doctor. She's a nurse, but she only works a few days a week." Rebecca smiled.

"That's her. I really liked her haircut, and she recommended the salon that I now go to. I never got her name though."

Beth was writing notes. "Barbie."

"For real?" The lady in the picture had blonde, wavy hair, plumped-up lips, and a significant amount of cleavage peeking into the picture. "Is that a nickname?"

Rebecca snorted. "It's very fitting, but her full name is Barbara Allen. I'll talk to her, give her your contact information, and have her invite you to the lunch as her guest."

"Why does she need to invite me?"

"The first scene of the season is the five cast members, you included, meeting and having a ladies' lunch. This sets up who's on the show. All the ladies have loose ties, like Barbie will invite you and she knows the landlord, et cetera."

"Everything is planned out ahead of time? I thought these shows were unscripted. Wait, we don't have a script, do we?" Maybe I didn't know how reality TV worked. I probably should've asked a few more questions before I signed up for the show.

"No, no script. Nothing like that. Barbie'll invite you. I'll send you a time and location where we'll hook you up with a mic prior to walking into the restaurant. But once you arrive, you'll just have a nice lunch and get to know the other cast members. That's how all these events will happen. You show up and be you. And you can plan events if you want. You can either do something here and perhaps give a tour of the resort in progress—"

"Oh, Sam would love that."

"—Or you can plan something in town or both. So far only the first week is planned out, but if you have an idea for an event, let Beth know and we'll see if we can work it in. We try to leave spaces open, but here is the confirmed filming schedule for you. The first event, like I mentioned, is a lunch at River Side Café, but you'll check in at eleven a.m. at an address Beth will send soon."

My head was spinning with information, and my stomach was turning. It could be nerves, or it could be all the vodka. "Okay." My voice quivered a little.

Beth stood up and patted me on the back. "Don't worry. You'll be great. You're going shopping tomorrow?"

"We'll probably be going over to Denver. Sami the Spender has her favorite malls she wants to visit. Any instructions on what to buy?" I chuckled.

"Actually, yes. White is tough to film, as are really small, busy patterns like houndstooth. It kinda vibrates on camera..." She trailed off as I cringed. "Don't worry. Just bring a few options when you check in so you can change if necessary. No worries. It'll be fine, but seriously, no solid white."

Rebecca stood and joined Beth. "We really should get going. Lots of work to do, but I'm thrilled that you joined the cast. If you need anything—"

"Contact Beth?" I followed her out of the dining room.

"Perfect."

I opened the door for them and shook their hands. "Thank you. Drive safely."

MELISSA

I was feeling regret. "Sam, do you think I spent too much?" We had spent four days in Denver and hit every mall, some twice. We were back in Fishcreek Falls to finish my touching-up process. As soon as we were done with lunch and drinks at the River Side Café, we were heading home to start planning outfits.

"Not really, except for the boots. Why in the world would you need so many?"

I gasped. "I needed each and every pair. They're so beautiful. Plus I feel powerful in them. Like I'm ready to kick butt."

She rolled her eyes at me and took a bite of her salad.

"Are you ladies enjoying your meal?"

A man had appeared at my left elbow. He was probably in his thirties, with blond hair and blue eyes. He had a pleasant smile.

"Yes, thank you." I smiled at him as he stared at me longer than was comfortable.

"Are you visiting from out of town or locals?"

My sister leaned forward to catch his attention. "Locals. The salad is very good."

He extended a hand to me. "I'm Malcolm."

My cheeks heated up as I shook his hand.

He continued to hold my hand. "I'd love to take you out to dinner. Are you free this Friday?"

Sam snorted. "It's a busy week, buddy," my sister interrupted.

"A week from Friday. Please don't break my heart, Melissa." He winked at me.

Sam rolled her eyes. "Oh brother."

"Sure." I struggled to make eye contact. I was flattered and embarrassed. People at the next table were visibly eavesdropping and giggling.

"Here's my card. Until then." He leaned over and kissed my hand then handed me a card and left the restaurant.

The lady at the next table leaned over. "That was the most romantic thing I have ever seen." She turned to her tablemates, who twittered over what had happened.

The waiter came over. "Is there anything else I can do for you?"

Sam pulled out a credit card. "No, thank you. We're ready for the check."

"It's been taken care of by Malcolm. Would you like me to box up your leftovers?" He grabbed the plates, and when I nodded, he left the table.

"He paid for our meal. How polite." It was like something out of a movie.

"Get that look off your face. He was sleazy when he grabbed your hand. 'Don't break my heart, Melissa.'" She used a dopey voice in her imitation before sitting up suddenly. "Hey, wait! How did he know your name?"

RYAN

"Ryan, Ryan, they ran a new article on the show." Becca burst into my office, where I was double-checking contracts and the schedule for picking up the crew from the airport in two days. This was what made the job so exciting. The energy was increasing daily. Once the crew arrived, it would be nonstop action for the length of filming. It would be easy to get addicted to the adrenaline rush.

"Look." She shoved the paper between me and the computer. "They're really excited about Melissa being added to the cast. They posted a picture and said it's 'can't-miss TV.'" She danced and squealed.

"That's great, Bec." I moved the newspaper off the computer.

"Ryan, I've got a great idea. Live streaming."

I paused in my reading. "We'd need a great connection, a place to host the video, and certainly more resources and planning."

"No, there's an app that will load it up instantly. We can announce it on social media. It's a great way to get people invested."

I sighed and pushed the computer back to focus on her. "Social media is *not* your job."

She pulled out a chair and sat down. "This is my big break. If we can get the network to go for the full season, then I'll be set."

I scrubbed my face. This was not going to work, but how could I let down my little sister? "Fine. First, you'll need network approval. I'll let you have one production assistant for social media stuff, but there's no room in the budget for anything more than that, and you can't let anything else slack."

She fist pumped a few times and did a little dance. "One PA is all I'll need. Woohoo."

My phone rang with an unfamiliar number but a local area code. "Hello."

"You have to hire Stacey back," a female voice screeched through the phone.

I didn't bother to hide my groan. It was Heather Beckett. She had sent several emails about Stacey not making the final cast list. "Heather, this is not up for debate."

She continued to talk, but I lowered the phone and mouthed to Becca, "Go get Beth." When I put the phone back to my ear, she was mid-sentence, but I went ahead and cut her off. "I'm not discussing this with you. If Stacey has changed her mind, then she can call Beth."

"Really? Why didn't you tell me that? You'll get rid of that writer?" Her voice was high pitched and nasal.

"The writer? Oh, Melissa. No, the cast is set, but Stacey can still attend some film events possibly."

"I won't film with Melissa. She stole Stacey's..."

I lowered the phone as Beth entered the room. I had planned to hand off the phone, but first I had to handle the threats. "If you won't film with Melissa, then we would hate to cut you, but so be it."

The line was silent for several beats. "I didn't mean it like that..."

I handed the phone to Beth and loudly said, "Beth, Heather's on the phone for you."

"Sorry, Ryan. I don't know how she even got your number," she whispered before speaking into the phone. "This is Beth. I'll help you with whatever you need." She rolled her eyes at me as she left the room.

Becca flopped down in the chair next to me. "Why'd you tell her that you would consider Stacey?"

I shrugged. "Why not? Stacey's beautiful, conceited, and richer than sin. People would love to hate her, or they'll want to be her best friend. Either way works for the show. She can be a friend of the socialites. If her lawyer husband stops fighting me on the contract, which is now much smaller and cheaper for us, she can have a recurring role."

Beth slipped back into the room and handed me my phone. "Sorry about her calling you directly. I think I have her calmed down. I never thought that summer working in a preschool would be so useful."

I chuckled. "Can we go over the schedule?"

"You got it, boss." Beth sat at her end of the table, which was overflowing with folders and lists and had a whiteboard attached to the wall behind it. "The first waves of crew will arrive tomorrow, and the remaining crew arrives Saturday. I sent out a confirmation email last night to everyone with instructions. We have the first crew meeting tomorrow night, and the rooms are assigned. Audio Jason and Camera Jason are loading up and driving out first thing tomorrow with two rental trucks of gear. I'm free all day in case they have any problems picking up the gear. They are working with two other guys whose names are written down some-where." She flipped through papers.

"No worries. I don't need to micromanage you. So long as you know, I'm good." I believed in hiring the best I could afford then giving them the freedom to do their jobs.

She smiled. "Thanks. We'll do gear assignment, setup, and meetings this weekend, then we'll hit the ground running Monday morning filming." Her cheeks flushed. "I'm really excited. Have I mentioned that already?"

"I'm glad to have you on the project. Reality TV is never predictable at the best of times, but this should be a pretty clear-cut job." Then I would leave this all behind and return to producing commercials, a nice boring, but predictable job.

CHAPTER FOUR

MELISSA

I fidgeted in the cold air. When I did, the microphone cord attached between my breasts tugged, and the mic pack on my waistband caught on my leather jacket. I had checked in ten minutes early after sitting in my car for another twenty minutes. They had approved my outfit—slim black pants, knee-high boots, white tank top, and fuchsia leather jacket—then hooked me up for sound then sent me over to production assistant Katie on the sidewalk corner to wait.

When they were ready, Katie would let me know, and I could go to the restaurant. I had turned my phone off completely, and without it I wasn't sure what to do with myself as I waited. Katie had given me a curt nod, pointed to a spot for me to wait then intentionally ignored me when I tried to make idle chatter.

Katie was young. I would've guessed fifteen if it wasn't for those pesky employment laws. I put her age at over eighteen for that reason alone. Was she local or part of the Hollywood crew? She had on thick rubber boots used for mucking out horse stalls or surviving in the pre- and post-snow mud that plagued the town, giving rise to the term mud season, a local term for the two transition times between the winter and summer tourist seasons.

The base and bottom of the shoes were hard rubber, while the uppers were neoprene. They were waterproof and warm but made your feet sweat. They were easy to take on and off and commonly sold in the stores around town. I had never seen this type of boots worn in Southern California, but perhaps she grew up around horses or bought them when she arrived.

I was feeling more relaxed and scanned Katie for other clues. She had a small tattoo of a snake on her wrist. The local high school's mascot was a rattlesnake.

I could've just asked her if she was local, but that would ruin the fun. I needed a question that only a local would know the answer to, and preferably it would include local slang to eliminate the chance that she knew from researching the town.

I'd always been intrigued by how people's choice of language revealed more about them than they intended.

"Katie, what times do the Pools open?"

The Pools was what locals called the Fishcreek Falls Natural Pools and Hot Springs. No one called it by its full name except first-time tourists.

"Eleven a.m. during mud season but only if you're a member; otherwise one p.m."

Bingo. She was a local through and through. Use of the term "mud season," knowing where I was referring to by the nickname, and knowing the unadvertised, membership-only opening time were all proof of someone who lived here. She stared at her clipboard, flipping through the pages then pressing the earbud into her ear as if she was receiving important messages. She must not realize that I could hear when someone spoke, and the line had been dead since I arrived.

Perhaps she dreamed of doing such a great job that they insisted she come with them back to California. She was cute. Maybe she even wanted to be an actress. I fell into a daydream about her life. Maybe she studied acting at the local college. Or she could be a ski bunny, getting whatever work she could since the snow melted. Perhaps she was on the verge of being a breakout in the snowboarding world, but her boyfriend died on the slopes in a tragic accident and she hadn't stepped on the snow since, the nightmares of the avalanche still haunting her...

I was so deeply engrossed in potential backstories that when the real-life Katie spoke, I jumped.

"How can I help you?"

I whipped around and Ryan was behind us, having snuck around a corner.

"They want you back at base camp. I'll take care of things here."

Katie nodded and marched off, her clipboard pressed to her chest.

"Good morning, Ryan," I said coolly. I hadn't seen him since he had been at the ranch. Either Rebecca or Beth had given me all the information I needed.

He chuckled lightly, the sound sending a warm tingle through me, and a smile snuck onto my lips despite my resolve.

"Morning, Melissa. You look very nice. I like your boots."

"Oh, thank you," I squealed before I remembered that I was supposed to be pissed at him. Oh well, a boot compliment plus the urge I had to burn off some nerves was a good enough reason to drop my frustration at him. "I wanted an outfit that I liked and looked nice but wasn't all boobs and body." I shook my head in disgust at the very idea of it. "I like boots. They're powerful feeling. Like I could kick butt in them."

"Did anyone tell you that they changed the name of the show to *Savvy Socialites of Fishcreek Falls*? Your parents should be happy about that."

I turned to him briefly. "Things are still a little tense around the house, but that'll help. Why'd they change it?"

"I thought about your parents' reaction to the name and spoke with our executive producer, who spoke to the network. They already had some doubts, so everyone agreed that 'sexy' was the wrong word."

"*Savvy Socialites*. I dig the alliteration. And I think I prefer to be called savvy rather than sexy. Good choice."

He smiled, his brown eyes crinkling at the corners. I would have made a comparison to them being the color of chocolate, but that was trite. Perhaps the tone of rich leather or stained wood with little gold flecks? My stomach did a few flips, perhaps from that shot I had taken from a flask in my car, and I tore my eyes off him to stare ahead at the restaurant. That was no better, as the anxiety of what I was about to do started building again.

Why had I thought I could do this? For what purpose? If I turned around and ran, I could make it back to my car and escape before anyone was the wiser. Then what? I bet that contract had some clause in it about mental instability. I could check myself into a psych ward.

"Are you okay?" Ryan leaned in front of me to get my attention

"Oh, yes, just... I'm fine." I gave him what I hoped was a

confident smile, though it felt like I was baring my teeth at him instead.

"Let me check something." He stood in front of me and examined my face, his eyes reading every inch of me.

The knot around my throat started to loosen as I returned the favor. I saw the family resemblance to his sister Rebecca. They both had large eyes and distinguishing features that were striking. I tipped my head, and my neck popped as the tension released from my body. Whatever he was looking for he had either found or not because he nodded once and smiled.

"What would you do if the cameras weren't here?" he asked.

"I'd go home?" Nothing sounded more delightful than getting out of there and going back to my safe, quiet bedroom office with a nice cool drink.

He chuckled. Maybe it wasn't so bad here either.

"I mean, if you were here to have lunch with a gal you met. What would you do?"

I caught his meaning. "Oh, I'd walk in there. Try not to look like an idiot while finding her in the restaurant. Then after I sat down, I would continue to try not to say anything stupid for the rest of the meal."

"You're a crack-up. I want you to go in there and do just that. Forget about the cameras, forget about the audience, and just be yourself. You look good, and you'll do great."

"I look good?" Our eyes were locked, and I no longer shivered in the cold spring air.

He opened his mouth to say something around his lopsided smile but stopped. "They're ready for you. Go crush it." He slapped my back.

I adjusted my purse and gave him a tight smile before walking away. I used strong steps that I knew gave my butt a certain wiggle that men noticed. I cut my eyes over the windows on the building next to me and saw that Ryan was still watching me.

I was all the way to the restaurant doors before my fear caught up with me. It was immediately clear which table Barbie was at. It stood in a far corner and had three camera people moving around it.

Barbie caught my eye and waved me over. As I got closer, I could see the tension around her eyes and the smile that was wider than natural. At least I wasn't the only one nervous.

"Melissa, I'm so glad you could make it." She greeted me with a kiss on the cheek and a hug.

I'd never kissed on the cheek other than my parents when I returned from a long trip, but instinct took over, and I returned the air kiss with a loud "muah" sound.

"Thank you for inviting me, Barbie." I sat in the chair she indicated to her right.

The cameras swooped around, constantly changing positions. I caught them out of my peripheral vision and did my best not to look at any of them directly as I had been instructed, but all my brain could focus on was the activity occurring around me.

"Tell me, Melissa. What have you been up to?" Barbie's eyes cut to the camera for a split second.

I opened my mouth then slammed it shut. The biggest thing going on in my life was that I was on a reality show, but once again the instructions I'd been given were not to discuss that. Don't look here, don't talk about that—this was far more challenging than I had dreaded. It felt like an eternity crept by while I tried to find my words.

A waitress approached and started sliding trays of food onto the table then took two pitchers from a waiter behind her. "Sorry to interrupt, but the drinks and food are here. These are lobster cakes and those are beef pot stickers from local beef. The drinks were custom mixed for us. The blue one is a Snowdrop and the pink is a blended pomegranate daiquiri. Make yourself a plate while I pour you a drink. Which would you prefer?"

"Thank you, I'll try the pomegranate one."

She lifted the heavy pitcher, and her hand shook as she poured. A little bit dribbled down the side, and a small blush rose in her cheeks.

I put a couple of the pot stickers on a plate, took the glass from her, and had a sip. "Oh, Barbie, this is wonderful, and the food smells amazing."

She beamed, and her shoulders relaxed a bit.

She took a sip from her drink. "I can't wait for you to meet the other ladies I invited. I think you'll really hit it off with them."

There were three empty chairs around the table, which led my brilliant mind to guess that there would be three other ladies coming.

I chuckled to myself and sipped the daiquiri then delicately tried one pot sticker. Sam had given me a firm lecture on not drinking, that reality shows used free liquor to lure the cast into behaving badly. I had agreed, but I needed something to do with my hands. I might have had hands my entire life, but suddenly they felt awkward. What had I normally done with them? Rested them in my lap? Placed them on the chair? Why didn't I know what to do?

Barbie kept leaning back in her chair then sitting forward as she quietly sucked on her blue cocktail. There was a bar across the backs of our chairs, and when I had leaned back, the mic pack had dug into my spine. We sat there sipping our drinks and sitting ramrod straight. What an enthralling show this would be.

The pressure of the situation weighed on me. I was desperately trying to think of a topic when Barbie put down her drink and squealed. "Mags! Pris!"

I continued sucking on my straw until an ice cream headache blinded me. My whole world narrowed down to the pain between my eyes as I rubbed the space between my eyebrows.

"You okay, Melissa?"

I peeked one eye open while the other twitched. "I drank a little too fast." I waggled my empty glass at her and delicately opened the other eye with a giggle.

"Let me refill that for you." She grabbed the glass from my hand before I could protest. "Melissa, this is Priscilla and Magdalena."

We exchanged air kisses before settling into chairs, all of us sitting up tall. Priscilla was a cool blonde, her smooth, straight hair pulled back into a chignon, while Magdalena had a bold, beautiful nose and riotous mass of curly black hair that enswathed her entire head.

"You can call me Maggie." She sat down next to me and smiled.

I was feeling much more relaxed, and the cameras no longer caught my eye as much. I was a natural at this, or maybe the pomegranate daiquiri was having its wonderful, alcoholic effect. Priscilla and Barbie were turned to each other, talking, and I took the opportunity to get to know Magdalena.

"Maggie, what do you do?"

She finished chewing the lobster cake and poured herself a drink. "I work with my family at Palma Glass on Main Street."

Palma Glass was a custom shop that made gorgeous hand-crafted glass bowls, vases, goblets, and such. I'd heard they did tours of their hot shop.

"Are you a glass blower?"

She nodded as she drank from her blue glass. "Yes, though I prefer to work on the torch."

"What's the difference?"

"Working in the hot shop is a family specialty, and a majority of what we sell like vases, bowls, large figurines are made there, but it requires working with my family. You work in pairs or more. I still do a lot of that, but my preference is to work alone. I use a torch to melt and shape glass into beads, marbles, goblets, that kinda thing. I have to work much smaller, but the trade-off is worth it to be able to make my own designs."

I nodded along. "I totally understand. Right now I'm living with my family, and it can drive you a bit nutty. I've worked with them as well, but we kinda stuck to our own jobs."

She gave me a knowing smile, and we giggled.

Barbie looked past me toward the door, her face having gone white again. I turned to see two women making a beeline for the table. "Stacey? I... I wasn't expecting... I thought..."

The table was set for five, and I had been told that I had four castmates who I would meet today. The two ladies approached the table and stood behind the single remaining chair.

One was a redhead that cut her eyes around the table, looking for a fight. When she looked at me, her nose flared, and I braced myself in case she charged. Next to her was a brunette with thick bangs and pretty blue eyes. She twisted the handle of her purse around and around in her hands.

The redhead spoke first. "I told Stacey to come. You invited her, and you don't just uninvite a friend to lunch." She bit off the words and dared Barbie to correct her.

Barbie looked past the table at the cameras while her mouth gaped like a fish out of water. I wanted to say something to help but still didn't have a handle on what was happening. I finished my drink instead.

Priscilla narrowed her eyes. "Heather, you know that is not what happened. You're being rude." She spit out the word "rude" as though it was the worst thing one could be.

"Don't boss me around, Pris. You know exactly what happened." She glared at me then berated a nearby waitress. "Can't you see we need another chair?"

The poor waitress raced to get a chair and brought it over. I caught her eyes, smiled, and tried to mouth "Thank you" before she raced away from the table. I had no patience for people who were rude to the waitstaff or anyone in a similar position. I considered it a sign of a major personality defect.

Priscilla was chewing out Heather about her tone. Barbie looked around the table with wide eyes. Maggie refilled her glass then picked up the other pitcher and refilled my glass. She lifted her glass and tipped it toward me.

I clinked my glass against hers. I reached for another pot sticker only to realize the plate was empty and snatched my hand back.

The waitress returned and pointedly did not look at Heather, placing one plate of food in front of me and the other in front of Stacey.

I made a point of saying "Thank you" while looking the waitress in the eyes. My dad taught me that it wasn't enough to say thank you over your shoulder; you needed to give every human the respect of looking them in the eyes when you thanked them. It was a minor thing, but I could see the tension in her face ease.

As she slid the plate of food in front of Stacey, Stacey poked at the plate with a fork. "Excuse me, what is this?"

"These are beef pot stickers and those are lobster cakes." The waitress slowly edged away from the table, looking ready to bolt.

"Pardon me, pardon me, do you have something from lower on the food chain?" Stacey's head wobbled on her thin neck like a bobblehead.

The waitress stared at her. "Uh, what? Do you mean like some vegetarian options?"

Heather caught wind of the conversation and took over. "No, not vegetarian. Lower on the food chain, please?"

The waitress nodded and left. When her back was turned, she rolled her eyes.

I snorted.

Heather glared at me. "It's rude to laugh at people's dietary requirements."

I took a long sip of my drink before I replied. I should let it go or apologize, but she had been rude to that waitress several times. "Requirements?"

"Yes, we are on a new diet that my nutritionist suggested. Animals high on the food chain pick up more inprocessabilities through multiple consumptions." She didn't stumble over the nonsense word in her statement.

"What are you talking about? Humans don't eat animals high on the food chain. Are you giving up tiger steaks and orca burgers? These have beef and lobster. Lobsters are barely above a plant. You can't get lower on the food chain without eating algae."

"Are you a nutritionist?"

"No, but if your nutritionist really used the word 'inprocessabilities,' then she's probably not one either. That's not a real word. She sounds like a shyster."

Heather threw her hair over a shoulder. "She went to school on a cruise."

"All the best scientists have studied on the Love Boat."

Maggie snorted on her drink next to me then coughed into her napkin. "Love Boat?"

Heather looked ready to leap across the table and throttle me. "You think you're so smart, don't you?"

"Must be all that high-on-the-food-chain beef I'm eating," I said.

The waitress edged back to the table with two more plates. One plate had pretzel rolls with hot mustard sauce, the kind with whole dark-brown mustard seeds, while the other was white meat on a skewer. "This is chicken. Will that be okay?"

Heather glared at me while replying. "Yes, that is lower on the food chain."

I reached for a pretzel. Cattle are true herbivores, while chickens are omnivores that eat insects. Chickens are probably higher, but I wasn't going to say anything.

Heather threw the pretzel she had onto her plate. It bounced off and landed in Maggie's drink. "That's it. First you get Stacey uninvited to this lunch, and now you are mocking people with dietary restrictions."

"I got her uninvited? What are you talking about? I haven't met either of you until today."

Heather stood up, her chair scratching across the floor and pulling around the heads of most of the diners that hadn't already been eavesdropping. She channeled her anger back at Barbie. "And you. You know I have specific food needs, and you didn't even ask about using our restaurant. I'm hurt. As a friend, you should have talked to me first about hosting at my restaurant."

Priscilla grabbed Heather's arm. "Sit down. You're making a scene."

Barbie, across the table, covered her mouth with a hand as her eye reflected unshed tears. "I'm sorry, Heather. I thought it would be an imposition and like..."

Heather crossed her arms with a smug smile. "I forgive you."

Maggie dug the errant pretzel roll out of her drink then refilled both of our glasses from a fresh pitcher. She leaned in to me and whispered, "I might as well try the pomegranate daiquiri, since you're such a fan."

"I'm thinking of diversifying my investment by buying a blender," I said seriously before taking a sip of my refreshed drink.

"You must like them a lot." She took a taste and raised her eyebrows in approval.

Had I really had three? That didn't seem right. The pomegranate had a tangy bite to it that hid the liquor well. "The glasses are pretty small." It would be much better in the bigger glass I had at home.

Everyone at the table was carefully picking at food and drinks when Priscilla sat up and raised a finger. "I almost forgot. I'm doing some charity work at the shelter tomorrow afternoon, and I would like to invite you all to attend. Can you meet me there at three to get set up?"

We agreed and smiled. I had received an email two days ago that listed the shelter as the filming location for tomorrow, so it was hardly a surprise invitation.

Barbie no longer looked ready to cry and was ready to wrest back control over lunch. "I thought we could go around the table and share a little about ourselves. I know that most of us kinda know each other in passing—"

Heather sniffed. "I know everyone that I want to know already."

I put down my drink. "Why are you being so rude? This is Barbie's lunch."

"You started it."

I inhaled to correct her but caught sight of Barbie shaking her head. I exhaled and shut my mouth with a clank of teeth.

I looked around the room and locked eyes with Malcolm. He made a beeline for me, and I sighed. I had enough on my plate at this exact moment without his overeager advances.

Stacey turned her head and spotted him. "Malcolm? What are—"

Heather talked right over her. "Are you a waiter? I need —where are you going? I swear this is the worst restaurant in town."

Malcolm had veered off, and I hid a chuckle. Heather's reputation must have stretched far and wide in this town.

Stacey nodded to Heather. "Mike hates it here. He has never let me come here before."

Maggie tore a pretzel roll in half and scooped some mustard sauce onto her plate. "I think it's pretty awesome here. Thank you for inviting us, Barbie. And I love the idea of everyone introducing themselves. I only know people in passing and would love to hear what everyone does for a living." She gave me a wink as Barbie bloomed under the compliments.

"I'm Barbie, your host. I'm a nurse in Allen's derma-tology and medispa office a few days a week, and the rest of the time I'm mommy to two beautiful daughters." She turned to me and nodded.

"I'm Melissa. I'm a writer, and I live outside of town on our family ranch, where we're building an upscale resort. I've lived here for a couple of years, but we've been coming up here every summer and winter for my entire life. My parents and sister's family live here as well to build the business. I would love to have everyone out to see it sometime." I had promised Sam that I would mention the resort.

Heather turned to me. "What do you write?"

It sounded like an innocent question, but nothing about her had been innocent so far. "My published work so far has been helping women and girls with unique and important stories to write their memoirs."

She set down her drink. "So you just record other people's stories like a secretary?"

"It's more than that. You have to carefully pick through the details to find the compelling storyline, like Lala the child bride who was later able to come to America to live with extended family. I offset her life in this horrible situation with her current life as a young college student to really drive home the contrast she has now with the unfairness of her past situation."

Heather sniffed lightly. "But you don't have any of your own work published?"

"Not yet. These things take time." The words were muffled around my clenched jaw.

She started to say something that turned into an "umph" when Priscilla elbowed her sharply in the side.

Maggie dabbed at her lips, leaving little traces of brilliant-red lipstick on the napkin. "I'm Maggie, and I also work with my family at a glass storefront and hot shop. The hot shop is out of town on 129 and the storefront is on Main

Street. Priscilla is our landlord. I would also love to have everyone stop by sometime. We can help you make a glass flower."

Stacey looked around the table, her shoulders all hunched over.

Heather let out a huff of air. "Go on, Stacey."

"Hi, I'm Stacey. I'm married to Mike. He's a lawyer."

Heather rolled her eyes. "Gee, Stacey, don't hog the conversation. I'm Heather. My husband Carl and I own the Trumpett Hotel and restaurant by the ski slope. We were originally"—she started to drone on about her background— her colleges, accolades at her sorority house—and when she started in on her early jobs, I zoned out completely.

I caught Maggie's eyes and giggled. I tipped my head at the pitcher then toward her empty glass.

Her eyebrows knitted, and she quirked her head to the side.

I raised my hand and was pantomiming taking a drink when Heather snapped, "I can't believe you're goofing off while I'm talking. I listened to you."

Heat rose in my cheeks, but not as fast as my anger did. "I talked for fifteen seconds versus the life story you're dealing out. There are memoirs shorter than that."

"That's it." She stood, and her chair flipped over backward this time. "I'm leaving." She took a step away from the table then turned to scream, "Stacey! We're going."

She huffed out of the restaurant, Stacey trailing her like a puppy.

Barbie hesitated on the edge of her chair before racing after them. "I'll be right back. Heather! Heather, wait up!"

Priscilla let out a sigh. "That's fine. I didn't want to introduce myself anyways."

I cringed. "Please do."

She fanned her hands across her chest delicately below her dainty pearl necklace. "I'm Priscilla Morrison, and my husband and I own several businesses in the Fishcreek Falls community. Like Magdalena mentioned, we own the store-fronts on Main Street from the historic movie theater to the community art co-op. I'm very involved with several local charities along with raising our two daughters and one son, though they are mostly out of the house now."

I pushed my plate with the remaining bit of food away. I had eaten far too much.

Priscilla pursed her lips and stared at me.

"Yes?"

"I probably shouldn't say this, but you shouldn't let Heather bait you like that. It's rude to fight at a luncheon. You should try to act like a lady."

"Who said I want to be a lady? She was taking jabs at me the entire meal for no reason. What could she have against me? We've never even met before."

Priscilla sighed as though I was a dense child. "We all saw the jabs, as you called them. You should have just ignored them. I look forward to seeing you both tomorrow. Now if you'll excuse me, I'm going to find Barbie before I go."

She left, a faint, delicate smell of expensive lady perfume barely wafting by as she passed.

Maggie sipped her drink. "Mel—can I call you Mel?"

I nodded. "Call me whatever you want."

"Great, Mel, welcome to the group. Don't worry about Priscilla. There is a reason we call her Pris. She considers herself the authority on etiquette, but she has a good heart. I think she likes you."

"That was approval? What's she like if she dislikes you?"

"She sniffs and looks down her nose at you. It's quite hilarious. What are you doing the rest of the day?" She set down her drink and checked her watch.

I hadn't given a thought to my day beyond filming. I had driven myself over from the ranch. "I'll probably call the ranch to see who can come get me." I gestured to my empty glass on the table.

"Our store is nearby. Do you want to walk over there with me until your ride arrives? I can show you what I do, at least the retail side of my job." She smiled at me.

My heart squeezed a little in my chest. Though I had lived on the ranch for several years, I didn't have any local friends. Casual acquaintances at church, the ladies at the medispa, the checkout ladies at the ranch store, the neighboring ranch, that kinda thing, but I had always been unclear on how to take it to the next step and start a friendship. This was a skill that I probably should have learned as a child but hadn't. "I'd love to. Should we wait for Barbie? I feel badly that her lunch went sideways like that. It was kinda my fault."

Maggie waved a hand at me. "Heather's always like that. She is used to everyone around her catering to her moods. Look at the way she treats her best friend, Stacey; bosses her around every second of the day."

How awful to be treated that way by one of your closest friends.

"How was lunch, ladies? You look lovely today, Melissa," Malcolm said, having snuck up behind me.

"Thank you, Malcolm. It was lovely."

He rested a hand on my shoulder and started to rub me. It was far too intimate for someone that I had met only one other time. I stood abruptly. "We were just leaving." I pulled a twenty from my purse and slid it under my drink for the waitress. I turned and abruptly walked straight into a camera person.

Had I seriously forgotten that we were being filmed?

Rebecca rushed over. "Hold on. I'd love to get footage of you two at Maggie's store. Maggie, do you think you could call over there? We could get a camera in to film you both arriving." She effectively cut Malcolm out of the conversation with her body.

I relaxed as he left. Perhaps accepting his offer of a date was a bad idea. He'd been charming, but now he was a bit smarmy.

"I'll call the ranch and see about having someone pick me up."

CHAPTER FIVE

RYAN

"Ryan! You have to get rid of her," Heather wailed while pushing her breasts in my direction. We were uphill from the River Side Café, and Melissa, Magdalena, and Rebecca were still visible inside.

I resisted the urge to roll my eyes at both her tone and her breasts.

She must have noticed me grinding my teeth because she suddenly changed tactics. "She ruined today's filming. I was doing my part to make sure you had enough good footage for the first episode—"

I cut her off. "Don't worry about that. That's our job. The only thing that you need to worry about is being your natural, charismatic self." I tried to smile as though I really believed in her positive qualities.

"Where are they going? Why are cameras with them? *Why don't we get cameras?*" Heather was pointing back toward the restaurant.

Sure enough, Melissa and Magdalena were standing outside while Rebecca stood with some of the crew. I nodded to Beth, and she stepped away to confirm the details.

Everything had started to go wrong last night when one of the male crew members started vomiting at one a.m. By morning a second crew member was also sick. We had moved them into their own rooms, hoping to quarantine whatever plague they had. This had left us even more short-handed than expected. All our careful planning had to be thrown overboard for an all-hands-on deck approach.

Beth signaled me over.

"I'll be right back, Heather. Then we can discuss you bringing Stacey despite knowing she wasn't invited."

Heather shrank back a little. I was still pissed about it, though it did make for a dramatic opening scene. The rule though was while the cast could stir up drama, it needed to be with other cast members, not production.

I stepped over to Beth.

Beth finished talking into her walkie-talkie then turned to face me. "Rebecca's holding the table at the restaurant in case they want to come back and talk some more. She was hoping you can handle that while she and a couple of cameras go over to Magdalena's store. Magdalena invited Melissa to walk with her back over there until her ride arrives."

It was good for Melissa to be making a friend right off the bat. They would help solidify storylines, plus they would be a fun pair to watch: young, pretty, and both single. Melissa's pants were tight on her legs, while the leather jacket kept showing glimpses of her figure underneath. Even from this distance, she was hot. I pulled my eyes off her and moved to return to Heather.

Priscilla was talking to Barbie, who was trying to explain to Stacey that she hadn't uninvited her to the luncheon for any reason other than it was a cast-only event and Stacey wasn't a full cast member.

Heather took a breath to start talking again, but I cut in first.

"We can be done filming today, or you can return to the table at the restaurant right now and talk. Which will it be?"

Heather's eye cut past me to where the crew had been then back to me. "We'll go to the restaurant." She cast her eyes to Barbie and Stacey and raised her voice. "Come on, you guys."

We walked down the slight incline to the restaurant. I used the walkie-talkies to get the camera into place so the ladies could re-enter the restaurant and sit down. While we stood around, a weasely blond guy came over.

"Excuse me, Ryan is it? I'm Malcolm. My family owns the restaurant. I have a date with Melissa this Friday, and I thought maybe you would want to film it for the show." He ran a hand through overprocessed blond hair.

"We don't film on Fridays." I didn't like this guy and started to step away.

"Oh, well, I can reschedule for another day. What day would be best?" He stepped in front of me.

"Does Melissa know you want to film the date?"

"Isn't it totally normal for reality shows to film dates?" he asked.

"If she wants to suggest it then that's up to her. Excuse me, we need to get back to work if we are going to get out of here on time."

We had only been filming a few hours, and already Melissa was the target of a guy looking to use her to get on TV. The whole thing put me in a bad mood.

I approached the crew. "Let's get started." I checked

that the cameras and sound were ready and signaled to the ladies to start.

Priscilla, Stacey, Heather, and Barbie returned to the table to sit down.

Heather definitely had an agenda. "I'm sorry that Melissa ruined your lunch like that, Barbie. I was just so upset at her behavior that I had to leave."

Barbie drew back a little, her eyes wide. "Uh, I'm just glad I could convince you to come back." She cast an eye to the two empty chairs left by Magdalena and Melissa. "I feel badly that they left."

"You shouldn't. Melissa's terrible. It's better that they're gone."

"Melissa's not that bad. You two just butted heads." Barbie weakly defended Melissa.

"Heather, don't start in like that. You were just as much a part of this as anyone," Priscilla chided.

Stacey sat, twirling her handbag strap between her hands and sulking. I hadn't been there when she'd showed up, uninvited. Beth had told me that Rebecca had approved Stacey being miked for sound. I hated that she had gone against our instructions but could admit that it made for good TV. And that was the real goal.

Heather was trying to explain why it was all Melissa's fault, and Barbie and Priscilla were trying to point out Heather's culpability without actually saying that Heather was a raving loon.

"Melissa is trying to push me out of the group," Stacy wailed, tears starting to pour down her face.

Beth had given the contestants instructions regarding discussing the show. Viewers wouldn't be interested in watching a group of ladies sit around and talk about being cast on a reality show. The viewers wanted to believe that they were watching a real group of friends interact, so instead of talking about the show, they could talk about the group of friends they'd joined or their new friendships rather than their castmates.

Barbie raced over and stroked Stacey's back. "You're still our friend. It's okay."

Stacey simpered. "Why did Melissa do that? Why does she hate me? I don't want to get kicked out."

Heather smugly smiled at Priscilla. "We won't let that happen, right, Pris? You invited Stacey to the shelter tomorrow, right?" Heather got up and went over to console Stacey.

Priscilla rolled her eyes then leaned around Barbie to look Stacey in the eyes. "Of course, you're welcome to come to the shelter tomorrow. I am sure the kids would appreciate another adult to read to them. Though, I think you're over-reacting. No one can break up your friendships." Priscilla looked disgusted by all the tears and emotions. She crinkled up her nose and passed a tissue from her purse to Stacey. "Here, why don't you clean yourself up?"

Priscilla pulled a full-size box of tissues from her over-sized purse. I had always wondered why women carried such big handbags. Priscilla's bright-purple leather tote was the size of a baby hippo.

Stacey sniffled and wiped at her eyes, smearing makeup into dark pools under one eye then dragging a black smear from the other eye to her hairline. "First Carl screwed everything up, then Melissa replaced me." She sniffled and burst into tears again.

Priscilla caught my eye across the room and shook her head in disgust. The other patrons, who had all signed a release and had agreed to act like they were having a normal meal despite the filming in the corner, were sneaking glances at the table. Priscilla noticed, and high red splotches grew on her cheeks. "Stacey," she hissed, "pull yourself together."

Barbie pulled a few tissues from the boxes and dipped them into her water glass before attacking Stacey's face. Before, Stacey's eye makeup had been smeared on one side, but now both eyes had black running down her cheeks and dripping off her chin. Her bright-red lipstick was smeared onto her front teeth, and her bangs were flattened across one eye. The more Barbie patted at Stacey's face, the more she resembled a confused raccoon prostitute after a hard night.

Stacey wailed, her thin shoulders hunched and shaking.

Priscilla looked at her watch then turned to Barbie. "I'm so sorry, but I have an appointment. I'll see you all tomorrow." She walked away, her mouth moving as she muttered to herself.

At the table, the conversation was going around in circles. Barbie was trying to cheer up Stacey, then Heather would wind her up again by saying how she wasn't included. I'd let them talk for a while longer just in case something was said then wrap for the day at this location.

I could get over to Magdalena's store, and we could film her introduction interview in the store with the glass vases behind her. If we left right now, I might be able to catch Melissa before she left for the day. After all this drama, I deserved to see her tank top one more time.

Then I could swing by the shelter and make sure everything was set up for tomorrow. And hopefully the sick crew members would be better by then.

MELISSA

On the second day of filming, I pulled the ranch SUV into a parking spot in front of the shelter and turned to Maggie. We already had gotten miked the first time we arrived, but then they had us get back into my car, leave, and arrive again for the camera. "Ready?"

"Yes, I am. Thanks for picking me up."

We exited the car, and I hit the lock button. "No problem. It was on the way. I hope we're not too early." We stepped inside, and Priscilla came over to give us each an air kiss.

"Welcome, welcome. I'm so glad you could be here."

The entrance to the shelter smelled better than I expected. Antiseptic cleaners mixed with a faint smell of animal that wasn't at all unpleasant. I'd had a dog growing up that passed away when I was in junior high school. By then my parents were travelling more, and they chose not to get another pet. I had always planned to get a dog after I got married at age twenty-five before I started our family around age twenty-seven. I was childless and unmarried, so clearly those plans hadn't worked out. "What exactly are we doing today?"

"This is a wonderful program that pairs local kids with cats and dogs at the shelter."

"And the kids read to animals?" I looked at Maggie to see if she understood, but she merely shrugged.

"Yes. Many of the kids have speech issues, trouble reading, or even just shyness, and animals are nonjudgmental. The children get practice reading, and the animals get a chance to be around kids, which helps with the animals' anxiety levels. Plus, many of the kids fall in love with the animals that need good homes."

"Oh, I see." I nodded along. "What will we do?"

"I thought we could read to a few kids, but they won't be here for a bit. Many of the dogs and cats are already in the reading rooms. Why don't you two walk around while I call the other ladies to see when they will be arriving."

A pretty young volunteer opened a door for us while offering her help. "If you have any questions, let me know."

Maggie and I stepped through the door to a long hallway of cement kennels. A camera person darted through the door behind us before it closed. Most of the kennels were empty, though bowls of water and food along with cards bearing dogs' names, ages, and breeds indicated that they had occupants somewhere.

We passed a few big dogs of various colors that raced to the fence and barked, startling me each time.

At the end of the row, one of the kennels held a small brown and white dog. He would easily fit in my purse, with a brown head, black nose, and white stripe down his snout. His body was mostly white with a brown splotch here and there. I expected him to race to the fence and bark like the others, but instead he slowly blinked and turned his head away.

I read the card on his kennel: "Bubbles, age: ~6 years old, possible terrier or Chihuahua mix." Written on top of the plastic sheath the card sat in was a number: one hundred and eighty-six.

"Excuse me," I called over the barks that echoed in the cement room. "Why is he so expensive?"

"What?" the volunteer yelled back, coming toward me.

When she was close enough, I tried again. "Why is Bubbles so expensive?" I pointed to the number.

"That's not his price. That's how many days he's been here."

"Oh, that's so sad." That was about six months. Six

months of sitting in here listening to dogs bark all day. I was already about to go mad after five minutes.

"No one wants an old dog even though he might have ten more good years in him. He's potty trained and very polite, though not a fan of kids. He doesn't bite or anything, but he's tiny and little kids tend to manhandle small dogs."

I kneeled down to get closer to his level. "It's okay, buddy, I'm not a big kid person either." I would have them one day and love them, but I didn't have even a passing interest in other people's children. I angled my head back to the volunteer. "I thought small dogs were popular."

"Puppies are but not older dogs. Plus, people around here want active dogs. Dogs that can go hiking and running. At a lot of places, they would've put him down already."

I gasped at the idea of his little fuzzy life being snuffed out. "You won't do that, will you?"

"We're a no-kill shelter, plus he's special. When his previous owner died, she left us a grant to start the reading program with kids and animals with the promise that we would personally find a good home for Bubbles."

"So all the other cats and dogs get a new home but not Bubbles." Day after day he lay there, missing his owner while other animals found good homes. Did he have dreams at night about being home on a nice, soft blanket then wake up in a cold, cement kennel? I wiped away a tear as a camera swooped into my peripheral vision.

My reflection in the glass of the lens distorted the scene it reflected. My head was huge on a tiny body, which increased the surreal situation.

The barking was dying down and Maggie had wandered away, but the volunteer hung close to me. "What do you do for a living?" she asked.

I stared at the back of Bubbles's head, watching his little body give a shiver. "I'm a writer."

The volunteer crouched down next to me. "Bubbles would make a great writing dog. He just needs one square foot of space, a patch of sunshine, and a blankie to be happy."

I nodded. I had figured that when I got a dog, it would be a big, goofy, bouncy dog, the kind of dog in every sitcom. Not a tiny dog.

"Why don't we get him out, and you can talk to him in the get-to-know-you room? Come here, Bubbles."

Bubbles turned his head and sat up. Stretching his neck one way then the other, he hopped off his suspended netting bed and made his way over. He held a back leg up off the floor and bounced on three legs.

"Oh no, what's wrong with his foot?"

The volunteer scooped him up. "We don't know. The vet can't find any breaks. He might just be sore. Follow me."

Maggie followed us out of the kennel area. "You getting a dog, Mel?"

I shrugged.

The volunteer ushered me into a room with a bench and some toys and placed Bubbles on my lap then closed the half door. It wasn't a real room since the wall only came up to my waist, but it would be a useful area to contain the dog. The camera loomed over one shoulder of the volunteer. Bubbles stared up at me, his huge eyes watering, then he proceeded to give me a good sniffing.

He circled around once on my lap and curled up, his head hidden under a back leg.

"What's going on? Is that a rat?" Heather's voice broke the moment.

Bubbles lifted his head, his tiny body vibrating in a growl.

I stifled a giggle. "It's a dog."

Heather pushed Maggie out of the way. "Of course you'd want a spoiled little dog like that. Wait a second, you're just doing this for attention." She glared at the camera pointed at me then focused her wrath on me alone.

I grimaced and wished her away from me. "I'm not doing anything for attention. I'm not even sure what I'm doing now." Bubbles licked a tiny paw and scratched at his huge bat ears.

Heather shouldered the volunteer out of the way. "Who says that I wasn't going to adopt that dog?"

Stacey shook her head, having come up behind Heather. "You can't have a dog. Carl's allergic to dogs."

Heather lurched over the half wall and flailed her hands at Bubbles. "Carl can take pills. Let me see that dog. I bet he likes me better."

Bubbles jumped to his feet, snarling and snapping at her. I wrapped my arms around him and pivoted away before her taloned hands could get within a foot of him.

He continued to bark, high-pitched yips, and she snatched her hand back. "Rabies! That dog is rabid and tried to attack me. Shoot him. Shoot him!" She clutched her hand as the volunteer raced over.

I pulled Bubbles to my chest. "He didn't bite you. You didn't get anywhere close enough." He growled at her, his body quivering, when a stream of tiny farts rolled out of him like a fountain. His name suddenly made sense.

Priscilla barreled into the room. This was her charity event, and she looked ready to take someone apart piece by piece. "What's going on?"

Heather grabbed her hand away from the volunteer.

"Melissa made that dog attack me. I probably caught rabies."

Priscilla's eyes narrowed, and her mouth shrank down into a little line. The volunteer had gone white. Priscilla looked at me, and I shook my head.

I stroked Bubbles's oversized head, and he whined and shook. "She grabbed at Bubbles and he got scared, but he was nowhere close to her."

Priscilla snatched Heather's hand and gave it a look. "First off, all the animals here are up to date on all vaccinations. Secondly, never grab at an animal. And lastly, you were not bit, and to imply otherwise is putting an animal's life in danger. If they thought Bubbles was dangerous, he might be put down. If you can't control yourself, you should leave." Red blotches appeared high on her cheeks.

Heather backed down. "No, he's just a nasty little rat." She glared at me.

Priscilla took a few slow breaths. "We're about to get started. Let's go to the reading room so I can introduce you to the students." She addressed me separately. "We'll go on without you. You take care of Bubbles."

I stared at Bubbles, and he stared back. My heart had stopped when Priscilla said they could put him down.

The volunteer returned to me while the rest of the group filed out. She still looked shaken, a weak smile on her face. "We have a starter kit with everything you'll need including food. Would you like to start the paperwork?"

Bubbles opened his mouth, a pink tongue lolling out to the side with a slight doggy smile.

I stroked the length of his smooth, compact body. My stomach felt like I was cresting a roller coaster, elated and eager. "Yes, I'd like that."

CHAPTER SIX

Melissa

Later that night, I puttered around my bedroom, marveling at the fact that I was a dog owner. Bubbles watched me from his new dog bed next to a small pile of dog toys, enswathed in a fuzzy blanket. By the time I'd finished the paperwork, the rest of the group had been done with their charity work.

Tomorrow was the solo filming, where the audience would "get to know our home environment" according to Rebecca, and the introduction interview, which she called a talking head. It would be me, and possibly Bubbles, in a chair, talking to a producer about my family, home, job, my opinions on my castmates, the first week of filming, and any other topic they wanted. It would be a few hours total. I bustled around my room, cleaning and organizing. They wanted some footage of me working, and since my writing desk was in my bedroom, I needed it to be spotless.

Bubbles watched me with his big eyes. He had sunk into the blanketed bed with an audible sigh after dinner and hadn't moved since.

The pet store had had a pet wash area, and I had given him a quick rinse to remove the kennel stink then dropped Maggie off at her store.

When I got home, I'd worried about what my parents would say, but they were surprisingly mellow. My mother had called him precious. Dad had acted like I was ten and informed me that I was responsible for any mess Bubbles made.

I also shared the news about the new title of the show, which I had forgotten to mention the day before. I may have let them believe that their input was primarily responsible for the change. It was a small thing, but a certain chill was gone from the house that evening.

I carried Bubbles up the stairs after taking him outside because he struggled to hop up the stairs with his little back left leg held off the ground. I would take him to the vet tomorrow after the interview to double-check that he didn't have a serious injury. He sometimes would take a step or two on all four legs, and sometimes the leg he held up would change. Perhaps he had bad hips or knees and took turns resting each.

I put on fluffy pajamas and prepared for bed. I tucked Bubbles into his soft bed then slid under the covers and flipped off the lights. The moon outside the window gently lit up the room.

I felt exhausted, but my mind raced. I was jittery from the adrenaline of the day. Normally I would pour myself a drink to relax, but I had used up the last of the liquor I had stashed around the room a few days ago. Why was Heather so awful? Maggie had filled me in that Stacey had been scheduled to be on the show but her husband had ruined the negotiation, but why was that my fault? The couples were close, with Stacey's husband's biggest clients being Heather and her husband.

How could Stacey stand Heather? It hardly seemed like an equal friendship with Heather bossing Stacey around and putting her down. Maybe Stacey was used to being treated like that. Her husband and parents might have been like that as well. Or her husband could have forced Stacey to pretend to be friends with Heather because of all the business Heather and her husband brought him. Stacey might snap one day and hit Heather with her car.

I chuckled a little at the thought. It would serve her right. How could any of those ladies in the group stand her? I fluffed up my pillow and rolled over. How quickly I was getting into the reality TV mindset. We weren't really a group of friends. We were all cast on a TV show, and part of the rules of the show were not to talk about the show. Kinda like Fight Club, the first rule of being on reality TV was not to talk about being on reality TV.

Beth had warned me, and I assumed others, that they couldn't use footage about us talking about the show, filming, production, or any of that; instead of saying something about the show, we should talk about our new friendships or joining this group of friends. It had been tricky, and a number of times I had been at a loss for words while trying to reframe my statements.

I had tried to say something to Maggie in the car—what had it been? I'd wanted to say that Heather was out of line for being rude since I had been cast on the show the same as everyone else. I had gotten the first half out then stumbled through the second half with something like "Barbie invited me the same as everyone else." It had reminded me of a surprise party we had thrown for Dad under the guise of having a quiet evening out with family, lots of talking around this issue and knowing glances.

A scratching noise drew me up in bed. In the moonlight, I could see Bubbles standing in his bed and scratching at the blankets, his long, thin legs pulling the mass of fabric to one side of the bed then adjusting and moving it to the other.

I flopped on my side and picked up my thoughts again to shuffle through them. Priscilla seemed nice enough if a bit formal. She seemed quick to point out improper behavior no matter the guilty party. That was a quality I could respect even though it made her seem a bit distant.

Barbie was a bit harder to pin down. She had seemed eager to chase after Heather when she had run off yesterday, and I had barely seen her today. The rest of the ladies had gone to read with kids and cats (along with a few dogs), while one camera had followed me through the process of adopting Bubbles, filling out paperwork, and getting instructions. I was pretty sure that some of what the shelter volunteers did was to show off for the cameras, but I couldn't fault them for wanting extra publicity for the dogs and cats in need.

The sound of nails clicking on the hardwood floor was soon replaced by the padding of paws across the rug. Though I couldn't see him, I could hear Bubbles walk over to the bed then circle it one way then the other. For a dog that weighed as little as the pretzel burger at the Irish pub, he sure was heavy footed.

"Bubbles. Go to bed."

The footsteps retreated and stopped.

Ryan, the producer, had watched me all day, but that was just his job. Every time my eyes drifted off into the distance or I stared into space, there he was, observing. My gut thought he was watching me. There were four other cast members—five if you included Stacey, who had showed up with Heather again today. Shouldn't he have been watching them as well?

The clicking of little nails came across the floor again, then the padding of paws across the carpet, until the delicate scratching of nails on the side of the bed broke the silence.

I was opening my mouth to send him back to bed when he whined.

I hesitated. Had he once slept on the bed with his previous owner? Was it torture for him to sleep alone as he had in the shelter for six months?

A whimper cut the air, and I leaned over the bed. His white fur shone in the sparse moonlight. I hung over the side of the bed, and he backed himself into my hand. I lifted him onto the bed and placed him near the foot.

He circled three times and curled into a ball. I yawned widely in the dark and pulled the comforter up under my chin.

I had really liked Rebecca and had hoped to chat with her at the shelter, but she had been too busy to chat, and in fact, Beth had maneuvered me away when I started to go over to say hi. Beth had dropped me off with Katie, the production assistant from the day before, who took me over to get miked. There was a hierarchy with cast separated from crew.

I rolled onto my side and knocked into Bubbles, who was a few inches from my face. He scratched at the top of the comforter then looked at me.

I lifted the comforter, and Bubbles rushed under it and all the way down to my feet then curled up next to me. His body warmth seeped into my feet, which were cold anyway.

I hesitated to move and slowly drifted into sleep, the images of a black camera lens chasing me to my dreams.

MELISSA

When I woke next, the moon was no longer out and my bedroom was pitch black. I was covered in sweat, shaking from a dream in which I had been about to fall into a sulfuric fire. My comforter was tangled at my feet where I had thrown it off. My throat was dry, and sweat dampened my forehead. My forearm brushed across a fuzzy body as I reached up to wipe it off. Bubbles had draped himself across my throat, his feet dangling on one side and his head on the other.

I pushed him off and sat up. My flannels PJs clung to my back. Bubbles sat up with only his white fur visible in the dim light. I pulled my top away from my chest, trying to fan cold air around my overheated body, when I realized there was an awful smell in the room.

"Did you poop in my bed?"

I flipped on the lights and leaped out of bed. The white sheets were clean, but the smell was awful. I pulled up the comforter and rustled through the wadded-up top sheet until I was sure nothing was hiding. Flaring my nostrils, I searched, but the smell was gone.

Bubbles looked at me and blinked slowly. It must have been the heat or the smell, but something had woken me up. I felt gross, sticky, and wired.

I grabbed a quick shower, really more of a cool rinse, and slid into a clean pair of pajamas. Bubbles was curled up on a mound of bedding, looking relaxed and none the worse for wear.

I chuckled at the situation and plopped at my desk. I hadn't written since I'd signed up for the show and felt the urge to get my thoughts down. Usually I wrote because that was my job, but the burning passion to communicate my thoughts had been a sensation that came and went. I started up the computer and marveled at how eager I was to tell the stories of Bubbles and all the weird people and experiences I had had in the past two weeks.

Beth expected a cast blog, telling our side of what had happened. She recommended we watch the show then give our reactions. It wouldn't hurt, though, to have some of my thoughts written down ahead of time. And writing would help me process my feeling. I opened a fresh file and thought about the day that Rebecca had come to the ranch, and I let my fingers race across the keyboard.

RYAN

I got out of the car and approached the house. The last trip out to Melissa's ranch had been tense, but hopefully this time would go better. Melissa's parents had been pretty upset the first time. Would they try to throw us out? Would Melissa? Monday had been pretty intense. I hadn't spoken to Melissa yesterday at the shelter, but the footage had been solid gold. Everyone loved a rescue story. What if Melissa was wearing that tank top again?

I pushed on the doorbell again when the first ring went unanswered after a minute. I double-checked my watch. "Beth, did you confirm with Melissa?"

This was the last day of filming before the footage was taken by the data wrangler on the morning flight to Los Angeles. I'd decided to do the interviews last so we could cover the first few days at the same time we got the basic information about who was who. The original plan had been for me to spend the day writing up production notes for the editor back at our makeshift office, but when three more crew members got sick, plans changed.

She nodded. "Yes, I double-checked with her yesterday at the shelter. Maybe the doorbell's broken." She stepped forward and knocked firmly on the heavy wooden door then leaned over to peak through the windows that ran up the sides of the door. "Someone's coming."

I tried to squash down the feelings inside me. Melissa was getting into my head in a weird way. On the first day of filming, she had looked cute in her boots and leather jacket, but it had been the haunted look in her eyes that got me when she stared off toward the filming site. I wanted to cheer her up. When I had and she walked off to start filming, hips swaying, it had about knocked me over. I shook my head as the locked clicked. This was a job. Cast and crew on reality shows did not mix.

The door opened, and I blinked. Melissa had a robe wrapped around her, mascara smudged underneath her eyes, and hair stuck out in odd directions. "I'm sorry, so sorry. I didn't sleep well, and after I fed Bubbles, I fell back asleep. Everyone else is gone for the day. Come in, come in." She gestured with her right hand, which was holding Bubbles, his tongue hanging out and eyes closed. One tiny paw twitched, then he farted. It started as a high-pitched squeak then stretched out into a loud, shuddering finish.

Melissa blushed. "Sorry, he's having some issues."

Even in her disheveled state, she was stunning.

I turned to Rebecca and the crew members, who were still unpacking equipment from the car. "We'll be back."

We pushed our way into the entry and set down the

gear. I chuckled as Melissa tried to flatten and smooth out her hair then waved a hand to dispel the noxious fumes from Bubbles.

"I really am sorry. Bubbles woke me up last night, and I couldn't get back to sleep, so I started working on the cast blog. Where do you want to film?"

"Where do you write?"

"I have a bedroom office. Boys aren't normally allowed upstairs—my parents still think I'm a teenager. But I got special permission. Come this way." She bounded up the stairs, waking Bubbles, and his sharp barks echoed in the entryway of the mansion in rhythm with her taking the stairs two at a time.

She showed us into a large bedroom with a mix of expensive and rustic furniture. "Give me just a second." She disappeared into her closet then into her bathroom, where the water started to run.

Beth and I left to show the crew where to set up. We grabbed equipment to haul up the stairs. Beth and Rebecca conferred, giving me a chance to observe the room.

Melissa's desk was near a window and was out of place in a room full of feminine fabrics and wood furniture. It was a heavy desk, with a laptop and one million sticky notes covering the surface. It was an area of work and creativity. Her laptop was open, and when I nudged the mouse, it woke up. On the screen was an open text document.

It appeared to be the blog she had mentioned working on. I read quickly before the bathroom opened, and Beth called Melissa over to get hooked up with sound. I eyed Jason as he pressed the mic between Melissa's breasts then pulled it off to adjust it.

"Okay, Jason, I think that's good enough." I walked over to take control of the situation. He hid a smile and stepped away, which irritated me even more. "Why don't we get some footage of you getting ready for your day, touching up makeup, putting on shoes, whatever, then you can sit and work at the desk for about five minutes." I turned to Bobby, our data wrangler, who was taking camera duty today. "Stay in here and get B roll of the room, the view and especially Bubbles?"

He raised an eyebrow.

"Bubbles is the dog. He has his own storyline." I didn't often get to say that. "If we're ready to start, Melissa, why don't you sit down next to Bubbles? Camera Jason, you follow Melissa, and Bobby, you're on Bubbles."

Rebecca rolled her eyes at me as she followed Beth, Audio Jason, and me into a far corner of the room, where we wouldn't interrupt the shots. Reality TV might have been dismissed as trash, but those that worked the cameras were experts. They had to adjust to moving subjects while standing out of each other's lines of sight. They had to be aware of everything in the environment and had no set script or blocking to follow.

Melissa sat on the floor, pulling a toy around for Bubbles to pounce on. He hobbled along on three legs, a back leg held off the ground. It was the perfect mix of adorable and pitiful. He let out a little yelp, and she comforted him before lifting him into his dog bed then wrapping him up. She leaped to her feet and took a swig of her coffee. The liquid was a pale brown from whatever cream or milk she had added. Then she went into the bathroom.

Bubbles watched Melissa leave. After a few seconds, he jumped up, landing solidly on all four feet. He narrowed his eyes at me, but when I didn't move, he raced across the room on four functional legs, jumped onto the desk chair and on top of the desk before shoving his entire head into the coffee cup. Beth stifled a giggle as Bubbles pulled his head out of the cup, coffee dripping off his chin onto the desk, and walked to the edge to peer toward the bathroom.

As the camera backed out of the bathroom, Bubbles jumped off the desk and ran back to his bed. Melissa exited the bathroom and went over to rub his belly to his moans of pleasure. "You ready to get to work?" She grabbed the coffee off the desk and took a drink then paused. Her eyebrows knit as she wiped the drops of coffee off the desktop with her sleeve.

This was going to look great in the episode. That little dog was the best actor in the entire cast.

She had just sat down when Bubbles barked and got up on three legs to hobble across the room and scratch on her leg.

"What is it?" She scooted her seat back and lifted him onto her lap. "Do you want to be near me? Does your leg hurt?"

She smoothly moved to her feet, carrying Bubbles. He looked smug, his tongue hanging out and his eyes half closed. She grabbed a chair and dragged it next to the desk then moved his bed onto the chair, placed him in the bed, and wrapped him in a blanket so only his eyes and nose were visible. The whole time the two cameras were swinging around her.

She settled in at the desk, and Bubbles locked eyes on the coffee mug through the tiny slits between his eyelids.

Melissa shivered slightly and wrapped her arms around herself. "You stay there, baby. I'll be right back." She got up and disappeared into the closet.

Bubbles shook the blanket off and smoothly leaped the one foot from the chair to the desktop and disappeared into the cup, deeper this time, so only the tips of his huge ears peeked over the edge.

Hangers rattled in the closet as Melissa pulled something down. Bubbles knocked over the coffee mug as he raced back to his bed, sending a puddle of coffee creeping toward her laptop. Melissa pulled on a cardigan as she exited the closet and was halfway back to the desk when she spotted the coffee and screamed, "No, no, no! What happened?" Then she raced into the bathroom. A rustling sound of towels being pulled off rods was audible then her frantic feet racing back to mop up coffee.

Beth was bouncing with glee next to me. "This is awesome," she whispered.

Melissa righted the coffee cup and dabbed at wet papers before carrying a dripping notebook into the bathroom.

Bubbles leaped onto the desk to check the now-empty coffee cup. He stepped on the towel used to soak up the mess.

Melissa was muttering to herself as she exited the bathroom, but she stopped as she approached the desk. Her eyes narrowed at the tiny, wet paw prints in coffee across her desk. Bubbles looked away from her as Melissa stared at him.

"Bubbles! Did you do this?"

Bubbles made his escape. Jumping off the chair, he ran across the room faster than a bullet on four good legs. Melissa gasped and covered her mouth as he scaled the side of her bed in a parkour bound like Spider-Man, ran to the pillows, and disappeared underneath them.

RYAN

I reached for the mouse and missed. I'd felt flushed earlier, but now even my hand was hot. The words on the computer screen swam in lazy circles as I tried to focus. I squinted while rubbing my stiff shoulders. Had the lights in here gotten brighter?

"Hey, Ryan, you don't look so good."

I looked up at Beth, who was working across the desk. My visions swam at the sudden movement, and my stomach heaved. I grunted in response.

She sat up. "Go to bed. If you get whatever is going around, then production will grind to a halt. We're already down too many crew members. I can take care of everything for you."

I drank the entire bottle of water I had next to me. It felt so cool. "No. Bobby has the first flight out tomorrow, and the production notes need to be at Ian's office before Bobby arrives."

"I already have a copy of those. I can send them over." She reached into a cooler and pulled out three fresh bottles of water. "Take these to your room with you. If you need any medicine, let me know. I'll grab it for you and leave it at your door." She edged away, one arm thrown in front of her face until she was at a safe distance.

I glared at Beth's overreaction. "I'll write a quick note on editing together the first episode." I looked back at the screen. The letters were fuzzy, so I rubbed my eyes.

"How about if you dictate to me and I'll get the information over to Ian."

I resisted for a moment, but the building headache between my eyes won out. "Fine. I'll give you the basics, and you can make it sound right. The episode would open with B roll footage of the town like the cowboy statue, the ski slope, the river, snow falling, then ease into Priscilla's interview in her house overlooking the town, then Magdalena's interview at her store, and Barbie's from her office that overlooked the ski slope. Next, the lunch up to the point right before Stacey and Heather show up, then insert Heather's interview. Add a note to make sure they include the interview clip about Heather and Stacey being friends. Then the rest of the lunch, with Melissa and Magdalena leaving and hanging out at Magdalena's store, just a bit. Then the rest returning to the restaurant to get Stacey's breakdown, smeared makeup and all."

I paused to let Beth finish typing up what I had said so far. Once she stopped typing, I continued. "Cut to the next day, the whole deal with Melissa adopting Bubbles up to the point she starts paperwork, cut back and forth between the ladies with the dogs and Melissa adopting and buying stuff for Bubbles. Add the next morning of Bubbles drinking the coffee, then finish the episode with Melissa's interview." I rubbed my forehead, feeling almost winded from the long speech.

My stomach gurgled, and I regretted chugging all that water at once.

"Got it. I'll make it sound good. Will they follow your suggestions or do their own thing?"

"I've worked with Ian's editing team on several other projects, and we've gotten to a point of knowing what the other wants. The finished product will be pretty close to that. You sure you don't want me—"

"No. Go. To. Bed." She was on the far end of the long table but still covered her mouth and shooed me away. "I've got everything taken care of here. Let's just hope you're the last one to catch anything."

CHAPTER SEVEN

MELISSA

"Mel, Mel, where are you?" My sister's voice woke me Sunday evening.

I was lying face down on the tile of my bathroom. The smooth, cool porcelain surface was wonderful on my fevered cheeks. I licked my dry, cracked lips and grimaced at the nasty taste coating my mouth. I debated getting up and finding some water, but the effort of sitting up was overwhelming. "Here," I croaked. Bubbles stirred on my back, where he was curled up.

The bathroom door creaked open. "Aw, Meli, you're not feeling any better?"

I groaned in reply.

"I just got back from Amanda's. *Savvy Socialites of Fishcreek Falls* was so good. The ranch looked gorgeous, and they included you mentioning the resort and the construction site. Bubbles was adorable." Her feet shuffled over to my face. "Do you need me to get Mom or something?"

I was actually feeling much better than I had a few days

ago when I had typed out a message to Malcolm canceling our date and asking to reschedule. I'd slept on and off until Saturday night. My big mistake upon waking up Sunday had been deciding that I was well enough to try eating lunch before going to Amanda's to watch the premiere, since we didn't have cable or satellite for the TVs in the house and the network wouldn't make it available online until Monday.

Not too long after I ate, I knew that had been a horrible miscalculation. And I'd been in the bathroom ever since.

"I'm fine," I mumbled into the tiles.

"Come on, Bubbles." His weight lifted off my back, then Sam pulled me into a sitting position and handed me a glass of water. "Drink this slowly."

I was a little dizzy, but once I was upright and leaning against the bathtub, I felt better. "What was the show like?"

"Really fun. Bubbles here was the star. I seldom say this, but you were right."

"Oh?" I pushed my hair out of my face then let my arm flop back to the cold tile.

"You told me that he was faking with the hurt back leg bit, but none of us believed you. I saw the video. He's a little sneaker. They used the footage of him hopping around on three legs every single commercial break. When he got up and ran on four legs to get the coffee, we howled with laughter. My sides hurt. And I checked online. Everyone loves Bubbles. They are making little memes of him with slogans like 'Bubbles's Oscar-winning performance' or editing movie posters with Bubbles's head on leading men's bodies."

She put Bubbles in my lap then flipped through her phone. "Here's Bubbles on the *Titanic*, and here's another of Bubbles's head on some guy from a romantic movie, you know, where they die at the end. Hilarious."

"Was I in the episode?" I grouched. I felt sticky and cold while also too hot. Whatever I had caught still had the upper hand.

"Yes. You were kinda hilarious, but we need to talk about your drinking."

My stomach flipped. "Don't even say that word."

She took a deep breath to chew me out.

I grabbed her ankle and gagged. "Please, I'll never drink again. If you say one more word, I may barf on your foot." I covered my mouth as my stomach contracted, and tears slipped down my cheeks.

Sam tried to pull her feet away. "Fine, no more. Please don't vomit. You were right about Hateful Heather and Sad Stacey. What a pair."

I took a deep breath, and my stomach settled enough to talk again. I chuckled when Sam used my nicknames for Heather and Stacey. "So you see why I called them that?"

"It is a perfect description. I might have even said that on social media."

"You didn't." I slid over to rest my head where the wall met the corner of the tub.

"I did, but people agreed. I was mad. She said in her interview that you were a nobody and didn't deserve to hang out with them. You're my baby sister. I couldn't let her get away with saying that you somehow were responsible for Stacey not being hired on the show. I got the inside scoop though. Stacey's husband, Mike, is a lawyer and kept asking for crazy stuff in her contract, and eventually the show dropped her for being too difficult."

Sam was neck deep in gossip. "Where did you hear that?"

"Someone local that knows someone that knows them posted online. Everyone local was watching and talking. I found the SSFF hashtag and got all the dirt."

"SSFF?"

"*Savvy Socialites of Fishcreek Falls*, the name of the show. If you use the hashtag, you can find all the posts, comments, et cetera. Did you know they're doing a live cast this week?"

My energy was already drained, and I no longer could even pretend to follow what Sam was talking about. I slowly tipped to one side, my feverish skin squeaking along the porcelain surface. My head lolled to the side. Nausea roared up briefly, and I swallowed hard. Bubbles crawled up my chest to curl up on my neck. "I don't know about hashtags or live casts. Go away. I need to sleep."

She ignored me and continued. "I signed up for the live cast. I'll get a little notification and can watch whatever they film live or watch it again later. They said the quality will be poor because they have to use a phone app to film it, but how fun is that?" She stepped up close to me. "Sitting on the bathroom floor is gross. Why don't you go to bed?"

I pushed at her ankle. "Let me die in peace."

A faint electronic noise came from my bedroom.

Sam pivoted. "Is that your phone?"

I still had my hands on her legs as she raced out of the room. Bubbles leaped onto the floor as I fell over. I closed my eyes on the bathroom floor again, listening to my sister's voice as she answered my phone. He came over and licked my eyelids before settling under my chin.

"Melissa's phone... Hi, Rebecca, I just finished watching the pilot. It was *so* good."

I heard her making noises of agreement into the phone as she listened to Rebecca.

"No, we don't have TV service in the house, and she's way too sick to leave. But I told her all about it. Wasn't Bubbles adorable?"

Her socks came into view.

"I'll ask her." She poked me in the side with her toe. "Mel, is your blog ready?"

I groaned and closed my eyes. I had whatever I had written a few days ago when Bubbles woke me up but hadn't added anything. "I need to edit it."

My sister walked away. "Let me check something."

Bubbles stood up and pawed at the neckline of my pajamas while whining. Once he had the material off my skin, he crawled down my top until he curled up against my belly. His tiny, warm body was a comfort, and I started to drift away.

"Mel, I submitted your blog. Rebecca wants to talk to you."

My eyes flew open. "You what? It wasn't done. My computer was locked."

She held my phone out to me and shrugged. "It wasn't locked, and I just popped the file named Savvy Socialites into your email and sent it over. Here," she waved the phone at me. "Talk to Rebecca."

I groaned and cleared my scratchy throat. "Hello?"

"Hi, Melissa. Rebecca here. I hear you're sick and didn't see the episode? Bummer. Lots of sick crew members here as well. It's going around. I had an idea about filming tomorrow. I know that you and Heather got off on the wrong foot, and it will be a long season at this rate. How would you feel about meeting with her tomorrow to try and clear the air? I was thinking eleven a.m. You come to the Trumpett Hotel lobby, we'll get you set up, then you can meet with Heather and talk things out. Wouldn't that be nice? Get on the same page so the fighting stops?"

Her words had rushed out faster than my brain could absorb them. "What? She wants to apologize?" That seemed out of character.

There was a long pause from Rebecca. "She'd like to talk. Would you like to talk to her?" She spoke much slower this time.

"I don't want to fight anymore." I was fading fast. "The conversation with my sister, and the vomiting all afternoon, has taken its toll. I need to lie down. Did I say that out loud?"

"Uh, why don't you give the phone back to your sister?"

I started to stand up, and Bubbles tumbled out of my top. "Rebecca wants to talk to you. I'm going to sleep." I passed the phone to Sam, who went into my bedroom to take the call. Standing wasn't going to work, so I dragged my body across the tile floor. Bubbles trotted next to me before sitting down to lick his crotch then lick my cheek again as I reached the bedroom. I halfheartedly batted at him for the disgusting habit, but he danced out of the way.

Half my journey to the bed was over, and I pushed onto all fours to close the rest of the distance. I plodded along, dragging my limbs like the Hobbits on their final journey to Mount Doom. As I moved, my foot caught on the inside of my pajama legs and pulled the elastic waist down under my butt. With each shuffled stride, they pulled farther down my legs until they were left on the bedroom floor behind me.

My sister caught sight of me and rolled her eyes as she listened to the phone.

I reached the edge of the bed, and Bubbles jumped onto

it as I clawed my way up the side and flopped onto the bed, pantless.

Samantha came around to my side of the bed. "Yes, I know where that is, and I'll make sure she's there and ready at eleven a.m. Bye." She lifted my feet, which were dangling off the side of the bed, and tucked the covers over me. "I'll take Bubbles out and bring him back. See you in the morning." Then she flipped off the lights.

MELISSA

The next morning, I reclined the seat and closed my eyes. "Sam, are you hitting every bump on purpose?"

"Here, have some ginger ale. Tiny sips. If you need to throw up, give me enough warning to pull over."

I didn't even want to think about the meeting I was heading to. I didn't want to fight Heather anymore, but the last thing on earth I wanted was to talk to her, especially today. I had barely remembered talking to Rebecca the night before until Sam came into my room and herded me into the bathroom to shower then bullied me into getting ready.

My outfit was best described as comfortable, and my makeup was passable at best. But I didn't look as bad as I felt, which was a victory.

I had woken up feeling mostly human, but that had started to slip as soon as my feet hit the ground. As we bumped and bounced down the dirt road toward town, I felt more like a blob of goo. "This was a bad idea."

"No, you'll be fine. We're on the highway now. We'll be there in five, and you can get some cold air on your face. You apologize for calling her a raving loon in your interview and say you want to start over. She apologizes for calling you a no-name hack. An hour max, then we can get you home."

"What did she call me?" I scratched Bubbles's rump as he pressed his front paws against the closed window.

"Don't worry about it. Your insults were far more clever. Why don't you rest until we get there?"

I closed my eyes and willed my stomach to relax as I took tiny sips of ginger ale. This meeting could go horribly, and it would be all on camera. Heather would say it was all my fault, and I would deny it. My stomach churned, and I wondered if I would throw up on camera.

Bubbles left the window and placed his front paw on my chest and laid his face next to mine while licking my ear. He had stayed by my side every second of the day since I'd brought him home. I had gotten sick a few days earlier, and he had slept next to me in the bed, wandering from one side of me to the other. He even slept on my chest, knees, between my feet, and next to my neck. Perhaps he worried that I was dying because he was completely bonded to me.

My parents, sister, or Amanda checked on me often and took Bubbles out to potty. They said that he rushed about his business and whined until he was back in my bedroom. I rubbed my fingers over his coat from nose to tail, and he groaned with pleasure.

The car swung into a parking spot, and my stomach lurched.

Sam reached over to squeeze my knee. "We're here. Come on. Shake a leg."

I grabbed Bubbles in one hand and the ginger ale in the other and followed Sam across the parking lot into the hotel. "Sam, wait. Where are you going? I thought you were going to drop me off."

She held open the door to the hotel for me. "And do

what while I waited? I'll just sit in here and look online to see what people are saying about the show. There's Beth."

I sighed and followed Sam. Within a few minutes, I was hooked up for sound and the crew was ready, but then Heather was busy.

My ginger ale was gone, and my stomach flipped several times. Beth was standing nearby, and I waved her over. "Beth, I don't know if I can do this. I might be sick again."

She studied my face, looking into each eye then down my body, before flipping her hand over and pressing the inside of her wrist to my forehead. "Ryan," she called over her shoulder.

I tried to stand up and straighten my shoulders, but my whole body hurt. I gave Ryan a smile. He had been the one to interview me for the show after they had filmed the coffee incident with Bubbles. I had expected a list of questions, but it had felt like a first date. He'd asked about my life and how the week of filming had gone, and before I knew it, the interview was over.

The network had made the episode available online, and I had watched it on my computer that morning. The interview of me talking to Ryan, who was offscreen, only consisted of a few minutes, but it had made an impression on me. My eyes shone and my smile sparkled, and I knew it was because of who I was talking to. Had everyone on set noticed how I lit up when I was talking to Ryan, or did they think I was just excited to be on camera?

A blush crept up my neck, and my cheeks burned. "Hi, Ryan."

He also searched my face. He had dark circles under his eyes, and his face was a little pale, but he still looked good. "You look flushed. Are you still sick?"

Beth nodded and replied for me. "She's burning up as

well. We need to do this fast." Beth looked between us before she took off to talk to the crew, ordering people around. "Where is Heather? It's now or never."

Ryan put a hand under my elbow. "I'm sorry you aren't feeling well. We'll try to get this done so you can go home." He took me over to a door then opened it and looked inside before escorting me in. "I read your blog. It's really good and the most popular by far."

"I hadn't really intended to have that all published. I was going to edit it and—"

"No, it was perfect. It sounded just like you and told the truth. You have a great writing voice for humor and comedy. Now sit here, and we'll get the cameras and Heather in here as soon as possible."

He closed the door behind him, and I put Bubbles down on the carpeting. I hung my head between my knees and groaned. I wanted to be home. A burp caught me unaware, and stomach acid burned the back of my throat. "I think I'm going to be sick," I said to Bubbles. The room was someone's office, and there must be a trash can. I walked behind a desk, passing a slightly ajar door, and found a can to drag back to the chair Ryan had sat me in.

I did not want to vomit. My stomach ached from being sick for days. The chair was close enough to the corner of the desk that I rested my forehead on my arm, and sweat soaked through the long-sleeved shirt I wore. I gave myself a pep talk. "Don't throw up. Don't throw up. You can go home soon."

I closed my eyes and focused on positive thinking. My stomach was calm. My breathing was slow and strong. I relaxed and imagined my body slowly floating away. Time stopped existing, and I felt better. The faint padding of

Bubbles's paws grew louder then fainter, letting me know he was exploring the room.

At some point the door creaked open, and a small part of my brain both acknowledged and ignored it. Perhaps I had been asleep, but not for long.

Sometime later, seconds or minutes I couldn't say, the door slammed open and Heather's voice screeched through my head. "I'm glad you came to apologize, Melissa."

I sat up suddenly, and the nausea hit me like a wave crushing into my sour stomach. I looked around, momentarily confused. The office lights reflected off the camera lens as the operators moved into position to film Heather and me.

I rubbed my forehead, where there were indents in my skin from the folds in the jersey knit of my sleeve.

Heather glared at me and folded her arms. "Seriously? You fell asleep? I have a very busy morning."

I covered my mouth and fought against my stomach. "Hold on. Give me a second."

The glare turned to disgust, and Heather stepped back. "Don't you *dare* throw up in here. Just apologize and leave with that gross dog of yours."

"Bubbles, come here." I called, realizing that he wasn't near me. He came racing back. "I think there is some confusion. I thought that maybe we could talk and get on the same page about not fighting. Like you could stop taking verbal jabs at me all the time."

Heather gave me a smug smile. "Me? You're the problem. You owe an apology to Stacey. And that's why I asked her to be here. Oh, Stacey." She smirked at me.

I waited and looked at the door through which she had entered, which stayed firmly closed, careful to avoid looking directly at the camera in the corner. Next to that camera was Rebecca, holding her phone with the camera pointed at the action, which must be the live broadcast that Sam had mentioned.

When Stacey didn't appear, Heather dropped her crossed arms and stormed behind the desk to a second door that was ajar. "Stacey! Come on." She disappeared through the door. "What's on—Help! Stacey!" And then her screams tore through the room.

I got up and raced after her, Bubbles clutched in one arm, the cameras close on my heels. The second room was another office, and sprawled behind the desk was Stacey, covered in blood. The pool around her of wet, red liquid had paw prints all around it.

I looked down at Bubbles. His paws were dark red, and blood was smeared all over his body and mine.

Heather was screaming and people were pushing into the room. Voices were calling instructions. The smell of blood hit me, and I doubled over to throw up in the corner.

"Melissa shot Stacey!" Heather yelled and barreled toward me. She ran into Rebecca, and they both went down in a tangle of limbs, cell phone, and hair.

I wiped my mouth and stood up quickly. The world spun. The last thing I remembered was a set of strong hands catching me.

RYAN

The office was going to be too crowded for me to follow Heather and watch the confrontation. Melissa had looked so frail and sick that I couldn't help but feel guilty for not sending her home right away, but I had a job to do.

Heather's shrill voice carried out into the lobby, where a

couple at the front desk turned around at the noise. I checked my watch and calculated that I could get Melissa on her way home with her sister within the hour.

A female scream cut the air, and I was halfway to the office before I realized I was moving. I pushed through the office, which was mostly empty. I pushed Jason out of the way of a door behind the desk and took in the scene.

Stacey was lying on the floor covered in blood. Heather was yelling and lunged across the room but ran into Rebecca. Melissa was on the opposite side of the room bending over to vomit next to a potted plant with a black gun underneath it. Melissa stood up, her face white and eyes staring into the distance, and started to fall.

I caught Melissa and scooped her up along with Bubbles, who was still clutched in one arm. The full ramifications of the situation couldn't be thought through right now, but production was definitely in trouble. I debated between taking control of the situation and taking care of Melissa.

I pushed back through the office to find her sister, Samantha. I found her in the lobby, which was filling up with curious people from the staff of the hotel and crew that were working outside the room.

Melissa was stirring in my arms, and I put her on a chair next to Samantha. "There's been a shooting, and the police will be here soon. Call a lawyer."

She nodded and whipped out her phone while resting a protective hand on Melissa, who still had the blood-covered Bubbles clutched to her chest.

As soon as she knew Stacey had been hurt, Beth had dialed the emergency line. The town was small to begin with, but the hospital was nearby, and the sirens were already audible. The doors burst open and paramedics raced in. I directed them to the office just before the police arrived.

The paramedics raced out the lobby doors with Stacey on a stretcher and one of the camera crew running behind them. Hopefully that meant she wasn't dead, though the amount of blood I had seen had been a pretty dramatic sight.

Heather, with her husband at her side, was screaming to anyone listening that Melissa had shot Stacey. The lobby was milling with people talking to each other, on their phones, or taking pictures or videos. Our crew was recording the scene or returning to the lobby after the ambulance pulled away.

Rebecca came over to me, her face white. "The police want all the footage and audio data."

I nodded. That made sense. I would need to gather the crew together in a few minutes. Nothing in our meetings had covered protocol for murder attempts. "Hopefully that will help them figure out what happened." I put an arm around her and gave a little squeeze. "Not like we would air any of that footage anyways."

"Um, about that. Remember our discussion about live casting some segments to get the public excited for the next episode?"

We had discussed filming the beginning of Heather's meeting with Melissa this morning. Rebecca had planned to use some app on her phone. The quality would be low, but it was just a teaser. "You can't upload that."

She shook off my arm. "It's too late. It's a *live* cast. Live. As in, people already watched it. And shared it."

"Rebecca! You have to delete it."

"I hit delete, but not until after it had been viewed a few thousand times. I couldn't help it. Once I realized what was happening, I ran for help and told Beth and got the crew out of there. Someone in the lobby was a doctor, and I got them. Would you have preferred I didn't do that and deleted the video first?" Tears rolled down her cheeks.

I blew out a breath and squeezed Bec's shoulder. "Hey, hey, it's okay. You did the right thing."

I turned to Melissa, still resting under her sister's protective arm. The police were bustling around the room, separating witnesses from looky-loos.

The police approached and asked to speak with us separately. Stacey had been declared dead on the way to the hospital, and it was now a homicide investigation. This was going to be a long day.

CHAPTER EIGHT

Melissa

I rolled over in bed Tuesday morning, and Bubbles repositioned himself in kind, nestling up under my chin. I buried my nose in his soft fur and breathed deeply, grounding myself in the moment. He smelled warmly of fresh, loamy dirt and green apples. When I had finally gotten home yesterday, Mom had bathed him with shampoo to remove all the traces of blood then slipped him into my room. I had slept fourteen hours.

My phone beeped for the millionth time that morning. I hadn't read most of the emails and texts, but this latest notification was from my agent. I unlocked my phone and read the short message asking if everything was okay and was there anything I needed from her. I really should have replied to her email about the secret project, but now I had a valid excuse.

I typed out a return message. "I've been dreadfully sick and yesterday was awful but I am hanging on. I'll be in touch ASAP."

Immediately after I hit send, she replied. "Stay safe. I'll talk to you tomorrow."

I breathed out heavily. I had bought myself some time, but not much. I had so many emotions to sort through and decisions to make before I wanted to talk to her.

There was a knock on the door, and Mom popped her head in. "Oh good, you're awake. How are you feeling?"

"Much better." I smiled.

"Ryan, the producer from your show, is here. He would like to check on you."

I scooted up in bed, Bubbles rolling down the comforter as I pulled it up to my chin. "Let me get dressed and I'll be right down."

"No." Mom stepped in the door, and her voice froze me in place. "The doctors said bed rest all today. You can come down to the family room then immediately back to bed. I'll get your robe." She brought over a robe from the back of the closet door. She scooped up Bubbles from the bed. "I'll take him outside." She exited, leaving the door wide open.

I grabbed the robe and ran to the bathroom. I wanted to run a brush through my hair and add some light touches of makeup. I breathed into my hand and decided that brushing my teeth was the first priority.

Yesterday seemed like a dream, far distant and unclear. After I passed out, I'd never felt fully coherent again. Sam had been by my side, as fierce and protective as a mother bear. She arranged a lawyer, and the lawyer had insisted I see a doctor. The police were eager to talk to me, but after I threw up on one of their shoes, they decided a doctor's visit might be a good idea.

They had taken my clothing as evidence, which fine since it was covered in smears of blood. I had started to cry when they swabbed Bubbles, thinking they were going to stick him in an evidence bag and take him away.

My confusion was the point at which the doctors got very serious. I missed most of what they said and did, but I did start to feel better a few hours later. Then the police talked to me, asking the same questions in different ways over and over. Eventually the lawyer made them leave me alone, and we all went home. I was supposed to call him if the police asked to speak with me even if they said I wasn't a suspect.

I finished brushing my teeth and going to the bathroom. I splashed some cool water on my face and swiped some mascara onto my lashes and some color onto my lips.

Heading down the stairs, I pulled my robe around me. I should have ignored Mom and gotten dressed anyway. Then again, thinking of her probable reaction, maybe not. I rounded the corner to the family room and saw Ryan kneeling on the ground in front of Bubbles, who was on the couch, and paused to watch.

Ryan was using one huge hand to roughhouse with Bubbles, tickling his stomach while Bubbles slapped his paws and playfully nipped at Ryan's hand.

"Most men don't like little dogs."

He turned toward me, chuckled, and shook his head. "I like all dogs. Bub has some terrier in him. Smart dog." He got up and offered me his arm to the couch then sat in a chair opposite.

I sat down and faced him. "I feel silly lounging around in a robe, but the doctors ordered bed rest."

"How are you doing? You were in rough shape yesterday."

I nodded. I had gotten to a point at which I was throwing up bile, and it hadn't been pretty. "I'd gotten beyond dehydrated along with the fever and possibly some shock. I think. Honestly, it is all a bit fuzzy. But today I feel much better. What about Stacey?" I was pretty sure I knew.

"She didn't make it."

"Do they know what happened?"

He let out a sigh. "If they do, they aren't telling me, but there are no arrests so far." He looked out the window and rubbed his neck before turning back to me. "Did you notice that Rebecca was there filming with her phone? We were going to try this thing where the viewers can watch what is happening on set in real time. There's an app, and when we are broadcasting, all the subscribers get notified. They can watch it live or rewatch it later."

"Sam told me about that." Bubbles finished sniffing Ryan's shoes and jumped into my lap.

"Well, Rebecca was doing that and broadcasted everything: Heather screaming, finding Stacey on the ground covered in blood, you throwing up, and Heather saying you shot Stacey."

I nodded. It made sense. "And the network canceled the show?"

I had mixed feelings about the show being cancelled. I'd had nightmares all night about police officers yanking Bubbles out of my arms and taking him away. Or cameras looming in my face while I tried to find my clothes, which was a new spin on the showing-up-to-school-naked nightmare I'd had for years.

"No, the show isn't canceled, but I thought you might want to bow out. It's unreasonable to ask you to continue on the show when Heather is telling everyone that you killed Stacey. The video is down, but several places grabbed a copy before it was deleted; gossip websites and news stations are showing a modified version." He avoided my eyes again. "It appears to be picking up steam. Heather has said that you are the prime suspect for Stacey's murder."

I rolled my eyes. "How did Stacey die?"

He shrugged. "The police released that she was shot. Someone did kill Stacey. And most likely, it was planned. It would be safer for you to pull out of the show. I'll take care of the network."

"So they're not asking me to leave the show, but you are?" He hadn't wanted me to sign up for the show either. Anger built in my chest. "Why do you keep trying to get rid of me?"

The muscles in his jaw flexed as he ground his teeth. "It would be safer—"

"No, I want to stay on the show! I want to be able to show people that I had nothing to do with Stacey's death. Heather is trying to set me up." I gasped—it seemed so obvious. "She *is* setting me up."

"She likes throwing out random accusations," he countered, but he didn't seem convinced.

"I need to clear my name. I feel badly for Stacey, but I know that her death has nothing to do with me, and I'll prove that."

Ryan searched my face before replying. "Okay. But not today."

"You're filming today, without me?"

"Yes, and you wouldn't have been invited even if you were well. Heather is organizing a gathering at Priscilla's theater for friends of Stacey."

"I'm not cleared to be out of the house until tomorrow. What about the rest of the week?"

"Only one day left of filming. We shuffled everything around to next week. We'll spend tomorrow interviewing people about what happened and getting their reactions. Magdalena asked about you."

I nodded. "She texted me asking how things were, and I let her know that I was okay but shaken up. She's said she would come over Thursday since you had asked her not to make plans Wednesday."

"Don't worry about that. Have her come over tomorrow. We can film you two talking about the week and do your wrap-up talking-head interview when you are done. I'll have Beth follow up with you both tonight to iron out the details. Make sure Bubbles is there. He's a fan favorite." He stood up to leave but paused. "Do one thing. As a favor."

After his repeated attempts to get me off the show, I was pretty suspicious. "I'm listening."

"Don't go anywhere alone, and don't be alone with anyone you don't trust."

I nodded. It was fair advice. "Can I trust you?"

"In this case, you can." He chuckled, and I melted.

I jumped up, scooping Bubbles into my arms as I moved. "I almost forgot. Let me walk you out." I walked to the entryway in my thick, fluffy, warm socks and scooped a piece of equipment off the sideboard on the way. "My mic pack from yesterday. In the excitement, I left with it."

He took it from my hand, his fingers leaving warm streaks across my skin where they brushed mine. "Thanks. I'll see you tomorrow."

RYAN

"Quit scowling. You're scaring the crew." Rebecca punched me in the arm and knocked me out of my thoughts.

"I'm not," I snapped at her. It was Wednesday, the last

day of filming for the week, and I was ready for a few days off after the insanity of Monday.

She chuckled and directed the crew to the front of the theater. We were filming in an old theater that Priscilla owned called the Fish. There was a newer movie theater on the far end of town, but this was used to showcase art, cult or independent films, plays, and special events. The room didn't have built-in seating, and the seats had been removed to put up tables and chairs. In front of the big screen, a small stage would allow people to get up and talk about Stacey.

A man came by carrying boxes full of wine bottles. Then three more people traipsed in behind him.

Rebecca laughed harder. "I guess you're a waiter today."

"What are you talking about?" I growled, then looked at the men again in black pants and grey button-up shirts. I had pulled the same outfit out of my closet this morning, hoping to look adequately somber and respectful. "Are you serious?" My black pants and grey shirt had a slightly different cut, but I would blend in easily.

"Why are you being such a buttmunch?"

I shook my head at my little sister. She could always get a smile from me. Who says "buttmunch" to their boss?

"Seriously." She stepped in front of me and looked up. "Spill it."

I jerked my head to the far corner of the room, where our equipment was piled, and walked over with her. "I feel uneasy about this whole project. I wish the network had cancelled. They should have after the murder and Melissa being slandered."

She searched my face with narrowed eyes. "I knew it."

"You knew what?"

"This is not about the show, it's about Melissa. You have

feelings for her." She jabbed me in the chest with a bony, pointy finger.

I smoothed out my shirt. "I have feelings about her all right, but they're all negative. She's stubborn and acting stupid. She should listen to me."

She chuckled. "She's not stupid. You're just mad because she won't do what you want her to. You *like* her."

"I'd like to shoot her out of a cannon."

Rebecca teased me in a sing-song voice. "You want her as a girlfriend."

"How old are you, Bec? And you know I have plenty of girlfriends."

"Oh please. Who?"

"I went to the breast cancer art show with Anne." There were a number of women I dated on and off, but mostly off.

"That was five months ago, and you left without her. She went home with an actor."

I shrugged. "She wanted to stay and network. And at Halloween, I went to a party with Natalie. And last fall, I went to the fair with Cindy."

"Cindy's not speaking to you since you refused to cast her in the show. And Natalie is dating a director." Rebecca crossed her arms.

"Tiffany and I went to a Fourth of July party."

Rebecca threw her hands into the air. "She got married to a guy last week. When was the last time you spoke to or texted any eligible females?"

I avoided her eyes. "Not too long ago."

She stepped into my line of sight. "Ha!"

"Fine. I haven't spoken to any of them since we started preproduction, but that's normal for me. When I am on set, it is all about work."

"That's not normal. You want someone in your life that

makes your life more balanced, not someone that you put on the shelf."

"When did you get all worried about my love life? Besides, my frustration has nothing to do with any alleged feelings. Melissa's sick as a dog and thinks that if she doesn't stay on the show, she won't be able to clear her name. This is supposed to be entertainment, not the kinda thing that can ruin someone's life."

"Definitely ruined Stacey's life." Becca searched my face and pursed her lips.

I kept my face blank and hoped that she would drop the girlfriend topic.

After a few seconds, she let out a sigh. "Melissa wants to clear her name? Okay, I think that's fair. Why don't I take her interview and her visit with Maggie? If you don't have feelings, then you won't care who films it as long as it's done, right?"

"Exactly. It's all yours. I'll go tell Beth." I caught the look of triumph on her face before I turned away. She was right, it didn't matter who did Melissa's interview. But a small sense of loss hopped through my mind.

***

RYAN

"Pardon me, waiter? Could you bring over another bottle of wine?" A stage whisper thrown over from the nearby table pulled me out of my thoughts.

I had decided to stand in the back with the equipment boxes. A rather large pillar dominated the rear fifteen feet of the room. I had been surprised when the caterers had set up a table on the far side of the pillar, where the view of the stage and most of the rest of the room was blocked.

The table was assigned to a group of women who hardly noticed when Heather got on stage and started the memorial. Instead, they warmed up with gossip about the local politicians and took to drinking wine like it was a competitive sport.

The leader of the group was a woman in her fifties or perhaps very well-kept early sixties. She had an impressive bosom that rested on her empty plate. Her frilly blouse drew the eyes to her foot of exposed cleavage. She had been pushing wine on her much smaller tablemates. One of the smallest members of the group was resting her head on her plate, but the leader pressed on.

She waved an honest-to-goodness white-glove-clad hand. "Young man, more wine."

A few guests at the next nearest table turned to stare.

I pushed off the wall and grabbed a wine bottle and corkscrew from the back table. "I'm not a waiter, but I'd be honored to pour wine for you lovely ladies."

"I'm old enough to be your mother," she corrected.

I flashed a smile and winked. "Beauties shine regardless of age."

Those that were still awake tittered and smiled and emptied their glasses to be refilled.

The lead lady chastised me, but she couldn't hide the small smile and blush that had crept up her neck. "Don't get fresh with me. And don't go far with that wine."

I went around the table, topping off their glasses.

I had always had a soft spot for women who reminded me of my dear grandmamma, who had passed nearly a decade before. One time, when I was young, I had spilled a large bag of salt on the grass. Grandmamma had gotten out a vacuum and removed as much of the salt as possible from the lawn. When spring came and a big circle of dead grass appeared, she told my father that a Great Dane had come by and peed on the spot. He didn't believe her, but she had stared him down.

She had been grouchy and difficult, but never have I had a more loyal partner in crime, especially after Dad passed. She had taught me growing up that anything worth having was worth working for, and that included women. A difficult woman could drive you to drink but was also the only one who could save you.

An image of Melissa and her insistence on defying my instructions at every turn flashed across my mind, and I squelched it.

As I finished filling the glasses, I returned to my wall to watch the ladies.

The matron took a sip from her glass and managed to empty half of it while turning to watch the stage. To her left was a lady in a hat with flowers. I hadn't realized that women wore hats anymore. Next to her was the sleeping lady then a younger woman who was noticeably listing in her chair. The table was rounded out with a lady to the matron's right wearing pearls as large as dimes.

Now that I had my attention on the table, I was able to pick up their conversation more clearly. The topic of local politicians was jettisoned for gossip that was of more interest to me.

"Can you believe that Heather brought this together?" The matron at the table turned to the two remaining companions who were still with her in mind and spirit.

Whatever was going on at the front half of the room was no longer interesting. Rebecca had that under control. It was unlikely this segment would take up more than eight minutes, and the event had already gone on for hours. I grabbed a chair and casually set it down to split the distance between the wall and their table.

Hat Lady shook her head. "She's meaner than a striped snake. She thinks she's so hot because she has the hotel on the ski slope, but I hear they had a bedbug problem."

Pearl Necklace Woman tsked and shuddered. "Oh, bugs, just dreadful."

Matron lifted her chin. "You know, I'm not one to gossip, but I hear that Heather's husband bought that hotel so he had a place for his activities outside the home, if you know what I mean."

Hat nodded. "I'm not surprised. I heard he had a dalliance with Stacey."

Pearl clutched at her pearls, which I was thrilled to see in person. "Don't be gauche." She took a moment. "I did hear that he was quite impressive... down there."

Matron sighed. "Like my dear Albert. God rest his soul."

I snorted. The matron looked at me and lifted her empty wineglass. I grabbed a fresh wine bottle and approached. After removing the foil and cork, I poured her wine right to the widest part of the glass, like I was taught.

"And who are you, young man who is not a waiter?" Matron asked as I moved around the table.

The gal who had been listing dangerously pushed away from the table, face white. "I'm... sick."

Matron shook her head. "She shouldn't drink so much. And speak up. Who are you?"

"I am Ryan Sethi."

"And what are you doing here dressed as a waiter?"

"It was an accident. I'm the producer of the show they're filming up there." I pointed to the front half of the room, where the crew was focused on the cast. "And you are?"

"Prudence Latrice. So you're the one responsible for the debacle of the reality show being in our dear town?"

"I suppose I am, Mrs. Latrice."

"Bah! Call me Prudence. Mrs. Latrice was my mother-in-law, the old battle axe. May God rest her soul. You should have consulted with me. Heather and Stacey weren't fit to represent our town. All that screaming and carrying on in the premiere. I've been here since the first families arrived. A *real* local."

I finished pouring the wine into the glasses that required it. "Had I known you were available, I wouldn't have rested until you joined the cast."

"Listen to the lies you tell." She waved a hand at me but didn't bother to hide her smile. "Sit and join us. I will tell you the truth of these ladies."

Pearl took the opportunity to leave. "Take my chair. I really should take my daughter home."

I pulled her chair out, and she tottered over to the gal who had fallen asleep at the table.

I took her seat at the table next to Prudence.

She gestured to her other side. "This is my sister, Chastity Lancaster."

I nodded at the lady in the hat. "Pleased to meet you, Mrs. Lancaster. I should have seen the family resemblance—"

"Save your compliments for Prudence. She's always had an eye for the young men."

Prudence gasped. "Oh, Chastity."

I chuckled. "Dear Prudence, tell me about the ladies of our cast."

Her eyes flashed as they landed on me. "I've seen your

show, you know. Not everyone is as they seem. Priscilla Morrison, for instance. She likes to pretend she is a proper lady and lecture everyone on etiquette, but I remember her getting caught with her panties around her ankles after senior formal when she was in school."

Her sister rolled her eyes. "Kids these days don't care about that type of thing. Most of them are living in sin."

"Oh? Even when she had a shotgun wedding that summer and gave birth a mere seven months later."

Chastity waved a hand at Prudence. "You're so old fashioned."

"If she wants to be free loving and wild, that's her business, but don't spend all your free time chastising other people for their behavior."

I nodded along. Priscilla had given me an earful on how we should have edited the first episode and had listed all the reasons. I had listened and said calming things like, "I'll bring your concerns to the editing team," which I immediately did. We'd had a good laugh about it.

Prudence continued when she saw my agreement. "We all have adventures in our youth, but recently they had to file for bankruptcy. She gave lectures on handling money before that. It was all very embarrassing for them."

Chastity glared at Prudence. "You know that—"

"I know. The Trumpett Hotel business was—"

"Prudence!"

"Fine." Prudence meticulously fixed her dress around her, adjusting the stiff lace around her neck.

The Trumpett Hotel was the one that belonged to Heather and in which Stacey had been killed the previous morning. I couldn't wait to pass on the information to Rebecca and Beth. Evenings, after our production meetings, we would chat about the cast. There was something magnetic about watching people put on a show and attempting to crack through the façade to the truth behind it.

"What about Magdalena Palma?" I asked.

"Lovely artists, her and her whole family. They've been in town for about a decade. We have one of their bowls in our entryway. Albert bought it for me when they first moved to town."

Chastity leaned forward. "I hear Maggie has some special work you can buy behind the counter." She winked at me.

Prudence looked at her gloves and carefully straightened the seam along the side. "I've never heard that. Barbara Allen is looking lovely these days. She was a homely little mouse when they moved here to open the dermatology office. She made a smart choice in marrying him. Not the brightest bulb in the box and frightened by her own shadow but harmless."

"I'm surprised she can walk without tipping over. She looks so off balance."

Prudence nodded. "Poor dear. Not everyone is as blessed naturally as I." She looked proudly at her chest. "Stacey is another one that is weak willed. Pardon me, was. God rest her soul."

Chastity lowered her head. "God rest her soul. Dear little lamb. Her husband, Mike, is quite a lawyer, best negotiator in town."

Prudence leaned forward. "Albert didn't trust the man. He thought..." Her voice faded away, then she cleared her throat. "He just didn't trust him. That's all I'll say about that." The firm set of her mouth told me not to push further.

Chastity nodded along. "That's how the hotel—"

"I thought you didn't want me to talk about that, but now you're bringing—"

"Fine." Chastity crossed her arms in disgust, the hat sliding down over one eye before she shoved it back. "New topic." She glared at me, waiting for the next victim.

I spoke with a casual tone. "What about Melissa McBallister?"

Prudence laughed. "She really gave it to Heather on your show. I know the family moved here and is building a resort, but they mostly stick to their ranch. They donated money to a few projects like repairing the sanctuary at the community church, the library when they were building an extension, literacy campaigns, lots of education projects, that type of thing. Melissa is very lovely. Reminds me of a young me, beautiful and strong willed. I was quite the catch."

"In your own mind," Chastity muttered just loud enough for us to hear.

"Ignore her. You should never believe anything about love from someone named Chastity."

"When Daddy named you Prudence, it was more to do with a hopeful wish than accuracy. You've never—"

"You're problem is that you've never—"

They bickered, their words tumbling out and mixing between them, though the tones were snippy rather than truly evil.

Heather came up to the table, a wicked smile on her face that never reached her eyes. "Dear Prudence, Sweet Chastity, did you enjoy the memorial service?"

Prudence and Chastity stopped fighting. Chastity took to fixing her hat, which hung askew after her war of words with her sister, while Prudence turned her full ire on Heather.

"You know full well that we could neither hear nor see a thing from back here." Prudence's face twisted up as though she'd caught a whiff of something that smelled off.

"I knew you wouldn't mind since you had wine," Heather said over her shoulder as she sauntered off.

Prudence grumbled and grabbed her purse. "Come along, Chastity. Let's find your daughter and get out of here." She paused briefly in front of me. "Thank you for visiting with us. You made this old lady a little less lonely."

"It was my pleasure." I looked into her sparkling blue eyes and couldn't help but smile.

"If you ever need anything, please don't hesitate to call. I'm in the book." She grinned up at me.

A younger gal came over to collect them.

The room was mostly empty. The crew was packing up the equipment. I found Rebecca and Beth near the front of the room and joined them.

"You guys will get a kick out of the conversation I just had."

CHAPTER NINE

Melissa

Wednesday afternoon, I pulled Bubbles into my lap and tucked my feet under me on the couch as Rebecca shared stories about the memorial event for Stacey. "Where did you get all this gossip?"

"Ryan met a lady and her sister that Heather had stuffed behind a pillar at the event. Locals, and they knew a bit about everyone."

"Did you catch their names?"

"I didn't meet them."

The cameras were mostly set up in the family room, which Amanda and Sam were redecorating to show off perfectly. The large windows looked out over the ranch, and they were debating what to move to make the background of the scene perfect.

Rebecca reached out and placed a hand briefly on my knee to get my attention. "How are you doing? Ryan told me that you wanted to clear your name."

"You know that I had nothing to do with Stacey's murder, right?" I took it for granted that no one really believed Heather, but I wanted to hear everyone I knew say it.

"Of course. In fact, if there's anything we can do to help, either on film or not, please let me know."

That was far more than I expected. "Really?"

"Of course, and I don't just mean the show, I mean me personally. Give me a call if you want to poke around. Oh, Maggie's here." She bounded off the couch and left the room, probably to get Maggie hooked up with a mic.

I didn't bother to get up to greet Maggie. I had figured out that it was awkward to repeat our greetings on camera after visiting for five minutes off camera. Instead I mulled over Rebecca's offer. What had she meant? Was there more that I could do to clear my name than saying on camera that I didn't do it?

Heather's main proof that I had killed Stacey was that I had been somewhere near the body when it was discovered. Maybe the blood on my clothing and hands wasn't a great sign, either. Did she really believe I'd killed Stacey, or was she getting after me like she had when she'd accused me of getting Stacey kicked off the show? If she really thought I was a murderer, then surely she would have quit the show.

"Hey, Sis, good luck." Sam ruffled my hair, then immediately smoothed it down before leaving with Amanda to get going on the never-ending pile of work for the resort.

Rebecca came back and got the cameras ready. "We're all set when you are, Melissa."

"I'm ready." I grabbed a toy to play with Bubbles.

The crew got into position, and only a small part of me even noticed. I had heard that reality casts forgot about the cameras after a while, but I hadn't believed it at the time.

"Mel!"

I dropped the toy and got up to hug her. "Mag! I'm so glad you were able to come over. Sit."

"How are you? Are you okay? What happened?" She searched my face. "You look pretty good, but you were pretty sick, right? Wow, you look really skinny."

We had texted a little but had waited to talk until the cameras were rolling. She'd said the scene would be more compelling if we had a real conversation rather than rehashing old details for the camera.

"Being violently ill will help you lose those last five stubborn pounds. I started getting sick last Friday morning. It was so gross. I was practically sleeping in my bathroom. I didn't even get to watch the show Sunday night, that's how bad it was. Sunday night after the show, I got a call about meeting with Heather to try and talk things out."

I had given it a lot of thought, and while I wasn't supposed to say that had production called me to set up a meeting, I also wasn't going to lie.

"Go on."

I took a deep breath and tried to pick my words carefully to make sure I followed the rules. "I agreed that I didn't want to keep fighting and that I was open to talking things out. But I mentioned how sick I was. We agreed on a time and that they would email over information in the morning."

Maggie nodded along. In a normal conversation, someone would ask who had called and set up the meeting, but she must have guessed.

"So in the morning, I felt okay and got ready. But it didn't last long, so my sister ended up driving me and Bubbles over to the Trumpett Hotel. When I arrived, Heather was busy, so they put me in an office to wait. After the car ride, I was feeling pretty sick. I put my head down and fell asleep. I didn't wake up until Heather came storming in then—"

"Wait." She held up a hand. "So you didn't set up the meeting, place, or time, and when you arrived Heather was conveniently 'busy'?" She put air quotes around "busy" as if she didn't believe it. "Did you know Stacey was going to be there?"

"No idea. Her name never came up."

"But Heather knew she would be there. I saw the clip on the Internet. She busts in, demands an apology from you, and asks where Stacey is, so she must have known Stacey was there somewhere."

I sat back and pursed my lips to think. The whole day was a blur in my mind.

She patted my knee. "Sorry to interrupt. Heather asked where Stacey was...?"

"Right. She asked about Stacey, and I said that I hadn't seen her. I hadn't even known she was supposed to be there. I realized that Bubbles wasn't around, so I called for him. He came running and jumped into my lap. Heather started looking around the room, then pushed open this door that was already partially open. She went through the door and started screaming. I got up and ran in there..."

Everything after that was fuzzy. I didn't want to say anything that would make me look like a liar.

"And?"

"I'm sorry. I can't remember everything clearly. I know that I saw Stacey on the floor and a lot of blood. I also know I threw up and passed out. And I remember Heather screaming at me, but that's it. I... I'm not a hundred percent sure of what happened in what order. I keep dreaming about it, and it's all jumbled up." A sob caught in my throat.

"Hey, it's okay. I saw the video, and it was really

chaotic. People were pushing and trying to help her. You went down pretty hard. Ryan caught you and took you out. Hey, look at me."

I wiped my tears and looked at her.

"I know you didn't do it."

The tears flowed down my face, and I realized how badly I'd needed to hear that. "Thank you."

She leaned over and hugged me again, squeezing and holding me for a long time. I sat back, and Bubbles crawled up my chest to lick my face. "Thank you. I know I didn't do anything, but with what people are saying..."

"Only Heather is saying that, but she is being loud about it. Maybe a few others, but let's look at the facts. You didn't set up the meetings. You didn't know Stacey would even be there. But you know who did? Heather. Her hotel. She was conveniently busy when you arrived, so they put you into that room. It's awfully suspicious."

"You think she did it?"

She shrugged. "Could be. She's a better suspect than you, for sure. It could be anyone, but really you are the least likely person other than me. Did you take a purse that morning?"

I pulled my head back in surprise. "No, I could barely dress myself. I only brought Bubbles." I ran a hand over his smooth coat.

"Where would you have hidden a gun? And if you didn't know she was going to be there, then why would you have even known to bring a gun?"

"Huh." I sat back.

"And her accusing you so quickly. So wrong." Her voice rose each time she talked.

"Yeah, so wrong." I was feeling emboldened by her

anger. Why wasn't I angry? I was the one accused of murder.

"Then what?"

"Then what what?"

She chuckled. "After you passed out, what happened? The video cut out after that."

"Oh? That is even fuzzier than before I passed out. I started being sick and couldn't stop. The police took all my clothing and swabbed Bubbles. He had stepped in blood."

She shook her head. "The video showed that when he jumped into your lap. His little paws were covered in blood. How did that happen?"

"When I came into the office, the door to the next office was partially open. I guess when I put him on the ground, he went exploring. She must have been shot already." I looked out the window. The aspen leaves shimmered as they flipped in the wind. Locally the trees were called quakies because of the way the leaves seem to tremble.

"She must have, unless you heard a gunshot?"

"I didn't hear a thing. But wouldn't someone have heard the gunshot?"

She shrugged. "I don't know enough about guns. Don't they have those silencer things for a gun, or is that just for the movies?"

"Not sure. I think they're real, but not like they show in the movies." Maybe it was worth learning a bit more. "Do you really think the police suspect me?"

Maggie hesitated. "Of course not. Not even a little bit." She avoided my eyes as she continued, "No. I'm sure they... No."

I debated pushing it, but I wanted to believe in her lie. "Who did it then?"

"I... I don't know. Come here, Bubbles." Maggie scratched the couch, trying to draw him over.

Bubbles looked her up and down and crawled off my lap to walk over to her then veered back to me and sat at my side.

"He sure is attached to you."

I covered his huge triangular ears. "He thought I was dying."

"Poor little guy." She reached over to give him a scratch on his tiny rump.

He squirmed one way then the other and stretched his tiny hips into the air to get the most from her fingernails.

"I never thought I liked little dogs. They're so yippy. But he's a pretty cool dude." She drew her hand back, and Bubbles crawled across my lap to scratch at a pillow.

I lifted it a little, and he wedged himself into the space between the couch, pillow, and me. His black nose and snout rested on my leg while the rest of him was hidden. A muffled fart sounded from under the pillow.

Maggie giggled. "Was your family surprised when you brought him home?"

"Yes and no. My dad dug out a book from the eighties on dog care, and my mother just sighed. I think she's given up on me a little. I know I would if I was her."

Maggie tipped her head to the side. "What do you mean?"

"Everyone in my family has their life together, and I'm a total mess. Mom's this well-respected writer, and Dad built up a super-successful business. They are all set even if they do nothing else in life. My older sister ran this huge resort and now is building the resort out there." I hooked a thumb toward the window and the construction site visible. "It will be a success because everything she does is amazing. My brother, the middle child, is an entertainment lawyer back east, and his business is taking off. He has these amazing clients. One of them wrote the book that last summer space movie was based on. And then there's me."

"What about you? You're awesome. I'm sure your parents are proud of you."

"Why would they be?"

"I heard you made a lot of money when your dad sold the company. A lot of people would be off blowing their money on hookers and blow or hundred-thousand-dollar nose rings or something."

"It was his company, not mine. I worked there, we all did, but he was the real brains of the operation. And yes, I could be going crazy with the money I made, but I want to do more with my life."

"You write. I bought one of the memoirs you wrote. It's really good."

"Thanks." That did make me feel a bit better. "I am proud of those, but they aren't my life's passion. I do them because these ladies have important stories to tell and I'm honored to help them. But... it isn't the same. You know what I mean?"

She nodded, and a funny look passed over her face. Understanding, sympathy, sadness, or maybe all three. I started to ask her what it meant, but she spoke before I could.

"What *is* your passion?"

"I want to write great books, like my mom." That had been what I'd told every person since I was old enough to talk.

"Really? Huh." Her eyebrows knit up.

"What?" I asked, a bit too defensively.

"I read one of your mom's books in college. It was beautiful and all, but I always pictured the author as this deep, serious, intellectual lady."

"And?" I narrowed my eyes at her a little.

Bubbles shifted out of his hidey-hole, crawled onto my lap, and shoved his head under my clenched fist.

"No, no, nothing like that. I mean, you're like crazy smart and deep, but you're also really fiery, funny, and fun. I'm sure you can write great stuff like your mom if you want, but I figured you'd write something different. Adventures or comedies. Something like that."

Frustration was building up in my throat. I wanted to tell her that I totally could write deep, meaningful stories. The type of books that they make you read in high school while digging into the metaphors. I was mad at her for saying, even politely, otherwise. All I had ever wanted was to be a great literary writer. I wrestled with tears that wanted to fall, though I wasn't even sure I knew why I was so upset.

She searched my face. "But what do I know? I melt glass for a living." She gave a nervous laugh. "Oh, what about your date? You had a date last week, right?"

There was an awkward pause while I fought to get my emotions in check. Finally, I managed a weak laugh. "No. This is kinda embarrassing, but you'll get a kick out of it. I got sick on Friday, so I texted Malcolm that we would need to reschedule because I was violently ill. He texted back 'Great' with several exclamation points. Then a minute later I got another message that it wasn't great that I was sick, but next week is more convenient. He suggested Monday afternoon."

Maggie rolled her eyes. "Not smooth at all."

"It gets worse. We had a busy schedule, and I wasn't sure what Monday would look like, so I said I would text him when I knew. Obviously, Monday went crazy. I was in the hospital or with the police the rest of the day, and when I got home, I went straight to bed. It wasn't until Tuesday evening that I even thought about it."

I grabbed my phone and turned it on. "I messaged him that I was sorry that I didn't get in touch when I said I would and that things were crazy and I might not be free for a while. I woke up this morning to this." I handed her the phone with the message cued up. "Read it out loud."

"'Have to cancel. I've joined a monastery.' Then there's a picture of a waterfall." She looked at me then back at the phone. "Is that a joke?"

"If it is, it isn't very funny. I know I don't have the best luck with men, but seriously, he'd rather join a monastery than go on a date with me?"

Maggie giggled and pulled her knees to her chest. Her thick wool socks were decorated with penguins. "That's okay. You don't have time to date him, not when you have a murder to solve."

"Solve a murder? No, I just want to make sure that no one believes that I could have done it. Besides, Heather will probably think about it more and realize how silly she sounds. And the police have all the evidence." It galled me to give Heather any credit or cut her slack, but I was on camera.

"No, she said it all over social media."

"But that was earlier in the week when she was still emotional."

"And this morning at the service she held in Stacey's honor. I wasn't there, but a friend was. She called me and said that Heather gave a rather impassioned speech about how we all know who did it, the one caught literally red-handed, the one who was seen on national TV trying to get

Stacey off the show and who, when that failed, found a more permanent solution."

"Are you serious? I heard about the event, but no one told me that." I found Rebecca in the crew and narrowed my eyes.

She grimaced and gestured at me to look away from her and back at Maggie.

I dropped my head into my hands. I knew that some people might believe her on the Internet, but this was getting out of control. "Why? Do you think she is just going after me like she did at the restaurant because she hates me, or does she actually believe that I could have killed Stacey?"

"I don't know. It really is bizarre. But you have to figure out what happened."

"Do you really think *now* is the right time? It's disrespectful." I cut my eyes to the nearest camera then away. I had tried to put a lot of meaning into the word "now" hoping that she would understand that I meant on camera for the show.

"Yes, right *now*. I don't want to freak you out, but some people are talking, and it will only get worse after Sunday. People are armchair Sherlock Holmeses. You need to give them evidence to know you couldn't have done it."

I hadn't thought much about the upcoming episode. Last I'd heard, the police were still holding onto the audio and video footage from the cameras, but the video that had Heather screaming that I shot Stacey was everywhere on the Internet. Maybe the network would edit that out, but more likely they would play it up for maximum ratings.

Bubbles pressed his paws into my chest and pressed his head along my face. He had done that several times in the past week—his way of comforting me was my guess. His warm fur tickled my cheek.

"You're right, Mag. I know that I had nothing to do with Stacey's death, and while I feel terrible about it, I can't just sit around and do nothing while Heather convinces the world that I did it." I felt bolstered and sat up, catching Bubbles as he tumbled headfirst down my V-neck and into my cleavage. His back legs bicycled in the air as he tried to gain traction.

"Count me in. What can I do to help?" Maggie's eyes shone at the challenge.

I shifted Bubbles back to my lap and tapped a fingernail on my front teeth. "The gun, right? Why didn't anyone hear it?" I sat back and shed my lightweight sweater onto the couch.

Bubbled leaped onto it, scratching and circling until he wedged himself under the warm, light fabric. The tiny hump of his body bounced around underneath it until he settled down.

I petted him through the fabric. "Are we sure she was shot? It would make a lot more sense if her murder had been silent, like a stabbing. Maybe she was stabbed with something round so it just looked like a gunshot."

Maggie shook her head. "According to the news reports, she was actually shot, and I know who we can talk to about guns." She pulled out her phone and tapped a bit. "When I first moved here, I went on a few dates with a guy named Ben. Super-nice guy, but nothing ever came of it. His dad owns a gun store on the edge of town, and last I heard he still works there. Let me call him and see if he's free."

She pressed a button and held the phone to her ear. "Hi, Ben, this is Maggie Palma... Good to hear your voice as well. I have a friend with some gun questions, and I wanted to know if we could come down to the store and talk to you... Got it. Thank you. See you soon." She hung up and turned to me. "We're all set, but we have to get on it before they close."

I unwound Bubbles from my sweater and stood up. He hobbled over to me on three legs and scratched at my leg as I stood.

I put my sweater back on. "Do you think your friend will mind if Bubbles tags along?"

Maggie stood up and straightened her clothing. "Just take him everywhere until people say otherwise. He's a celebrity now."

I turned and caught a glimpse of the camera crew. "Oops. Rebecca, are we good? Sorry, I kind of forgot about you."

"You should be, but hold on a second." She turned to give instructions to the crew, and half of them started packing up.

Jason, one of the audio techs, came over to remove Maggie's mic, but Rebecca stopped him. "Leave her miked. I was thinking that after we film Melissa's interview, then a few of us could go with them to the gun store and film it, just in case."

He shrugged. "No problem. I'll grab my stuff."

Beth came up and pulled Rebecca aside. "Bobby's flight is tonight, remember? And you still need to film Melissa's talking-head interview."

"We can do the interview right now. It will be pretty quick, since Melissa just went over what happened Monday with Magdalena. The footage from the gun store we won't send out with Bobby. Once we're done filming here, you can take everything back and get what we shot. I want to go with them to the gun store in case there is anything we end up wanting for the future. You never know." She turned back to us. "Magdalena, can you call your friend again and see if he would sign a waiver to appear on camera?"

CHAPTER TEN

RYAN

I pulled into the parking lot of Fishcreek Falls Firearms Wednesday evening and cursed my sister for going off schedule and setting up additional filming without telling me.

Pulling into an empty spot next to the other production vehicle, I took a few deep breaths before approaching the front of the store. The door was locked, with a handwritten sign in the window behind the metal bars blocking the glass. The sign said that the store was closed early today. Pressing my face against the glass, I could see Rebecca hanging near the door with a large man in a plaid shirt.

The man caught me looking at him and poked at the sign. I pointed at Rebecca, and he nudged her. She turned and flinched when she saw me. Good. She had more than a little explaining to do.

The man unlocked the door. "Sorry, man, I didn't realize you were with the show."

"I'm Ryan, the producer." I shook the man's hand and

quickly pulled Rebecca aside. "What is going on? This was *not* on the schedule."

Rebecca clasped her hands in front of her. "Please don't be mad. This is *so* good. I mean, we don't need this footage, but what if? What if this clears Melissa? Don't you want her to be proven innocent?" She bounced on her toes, looking like the teenage younger sister who had begged me to show her how my camera worked.

I knew I would give in, and so did she. I just growled and walked over to watch Melissa and Magdalena talk to a man behind the counter.

Bubbles was sniffing around Melissa's feet. He followed his nose over until he sniffed at my feet instead. He scratched at my shoe. I scooped him off the ground and held him in my arm. The funny little dog licked at my thumb then laid his head on my hand.

The feedback we had gotten about the first episode was that Bubbles was a highlight. Not only the story of his adoption but the scene where the audience discovered that he was faking his rear leg injury. He had won over the hearts of the viewers nationwide.

The socialites were not proving so lucky. The opinions about Barbie, Priscilla, and Magdalena were pleasant but not particularly interested. The focus of the comments was on Heather, Stacey, and Melissa, with opinion sharply splitting between the two factions. Stacey was not in the opening credits, which comprised a scene featuring each lady superimposed in front of a view of the town covered in snow, holding a crystal snowflake, while her name appeared on the screen in curly gold script.

Stacey wasn't a main cast member but had appeared in the entire first episode. Many people felt bad for Stacey and thought Heather was defending her friend. Others simply thought that Melissa was rude. An almost equal number of fans had sided with Melissa and thought she had been unfairly targeted by Heather. The two sides were in a dead heat until Bubbles showed up; then the animal lovers were strongly in favor of Melissa.

It was difficult for me to see the support for Heather and Stacey after the difficulty they both had caused production, and me especially, but Ian had insisted it was good. Apparently fights that strongly split the viewers were good for ratings. From sports to politics to reality TV, the nation's favorite pastime was picking sides.

After the video Monday at the hotel, Melissa's side seemed larger, but Heather's side was louder and more vicious, just as she was. Katie, the production assistant, was keeping an eye on social media, and there was several loons screaming to arrest Melissa. Not only had I dragged her into the public eye, but I felt responsible for pinning a target on her back.

At the counter, a man had been explaining how a silencer, or suppressor, worked on a gun and the possible reasons no one had heard the shot. He reached behind the counter and pulled out a stack of pictures and laid them across the glass countertop. "By any chance did the gun at the scene look like any of these? And was there a bookcase in the room that looked like this?"

Magdalena looked at Melissa, who shook her head. "Maybe? I think there was a bookcase. I never saw the gun."

I leaned over to Rebecca. "We aren't using this footage."

I stepped up next to Melissa to look at the photographs. When I had arranged filming at the hotel, I had been in the office where Stacey was found. The bookcase in the office had been odd and caught my attention. Usually the sides of a bookcase are thin, but the bookcase in the office matched the one in the picture. Its sides were at least as wide as the palm of my hand. I had noticed and thought it a waste of space and overkill unless someone was planning on storing raw ore in the bookcase.

I had also seen the gun when I caught Melissa as she fainted. She had felt light as a feather when I scooped her and Bubbles up. The gun had been placed or had fallen behind a potted plant.

Melissa looked startled when I stood next to her. I had crossed the line from behind the camera to in front of it.

I shook my head. "Don't worry about it. We're not using this." I looked more closely at the gun pictures. I was no expert, but I'd shot enough to be familiar with the options in front of me. I pointed to the middle gun. "I can't say for sure that this gun was the one in the office, but if it wasn't this gun, it was something very similar. And this bookcase was definitely in the office when I was there a couple weeks ago. I noticed how odd the sides were, like too thick. Pretty sure it was still there Monday. Why do you have a picture of it?" I extended my hand over the counter. "Oh, sorry, I'm Ryan. I'm the producer."

He clasped my hand. "Nice to meet you, man. I'm Ben. I made this bookcase." He pointed to the bookcase in the picture, which was empty except for a single book, *War and Peace*, lying on its side on the middle shelf. "That book is a hinge. When you lift the book, a latch unhooks, and the side opens to reveal a gun compartment. These guns are all ones I transferred for Carl Beckett. In order for someone to buy a silencer, it has to be transferred through a gun store like ours."

He flipped the picture to reveal a second image with the bookcase's side opened. A series of hooks was revealed. It would be an excellent place to hide any number of guns, but it was suspicious that he had just the right pile of pictures lying around.

Melissa gasped. "That gun belongs to Carl, Heather's husband. No wonder she's so eager to blame me."

"Hold on." I scratched my chin as they waited for me to speak. "Wouldn't I have heard a gunshot? We miked up Stacey, and she was in that office for a while before Melissa showed up."

Ben leaned back, and his voice changed tone. It went from a casual conversation to instructor mode. "Though these"—he pointed to the black canister attached to the barrel of the gun in the picture—"are legally called silencers, they do not make guns silent, and that's why a lot of people prefer to call them suppressors. They suppress the sound from the typical gunshot noise that can cause hearing damage down to a crack that won't."

"How loud?"

He leaned back and looked at the ceiling for a few moments. "I can't say for sure without testing, but..." He thought for a bit before crossing his arms and continuing. "I feel pretty confident in saying that if the office door was closed, then those in the lobby probably would have heard the gunshot but not necessarily known what it was. In the lobby or outside, it would have sounded like a book dropping, a door slamming, a car backfiring, or maybe luggage falling over and hitting the floor. I bet people heard it but didn't think anything of it."

Melissa looked a little pale. "Could someone have shot her while I was in the next office over?"

"Were you listening to music on headphones? Did you hear anything?"

She shook her head. "No music, and it was quiet enough that I fell asleep waiting."

"Then it probably happened before you were in the room. If Stacey had a microphone on, any chance the murder was recorded?"

I rubbed the back of my neck in frustration. I'd had the same thought. "Maybe." Both Magdalena and Melissa turned to me in shock while I chuckled. "The audio was recording, but the guys had taken off their headphones to help with setup and didn't hear anything. When the police arrived, they took everything into evidence. Hopefully, they're using it to find the real killer."

Melissa was still a little pale but had a determined set to her mouth.

Magdalena grabbed her hand and squeezed. "This is the kinda proof we need. That could be Carl's gun with a silencer, and he had a secret gun compartment. He's the most likely suspect, not you."

I took an assessment of Ben. He seemed a bit too pleased to pin the blame on Carl. "Why do you have these pictures, and why show them to us? Have you told the police?"

Ben looked at me, his face turning red, and stammered. "Well, no, not yet. I sold him the guns and built the book-case then installed it in his office."

"And you're so willing to tell us..." I didn't trust information that came so easily.

He blew out a sigh. "Carl never paid me for the book-case. Said that it wasn't the right color, but he kept the book-case all right."

"Why didn't you take him to court?"

"His sleazy lawyer, Stacey's husband, Mike Rickman, called me and threatened to bury me in legal fees if I tried it. We'd discussed some minor changes to the bookcase over the phone and didn't really have a contract, which I know was a horrible idea, but I didn't suspect he would be so slimy about it. My father has never had something like that happen in all the years he's owned the store. I'm sure we could have won the case eventually, but we don't have the money to pay for a lawyer to fight it for years."

"So Mike Rickman also knew about the bookcase and its secret compartment?"

He nodded. "Definitely."

Next to me, Melissa reached over to scratch Bubbles on the back, her long fingernails tickling my skin. "Probably Heather as well?"

"Actually, yes. I remember her coming into the office. I'm not even sure that it was legal for him to keep a silencer in the bookcase compartment. A silencer needs to be with its paperwork and owner at all times. The bookcase has a latch, but that doesn't qualify it as a gun safe. I warned him about that. Especially with the cleaning staff around."

Melissa reached over and took Bubbles from my arms. "Because they might have figured out the secret compartment?"

Bubbles sprawled on his back in the crook of her arm, all four feet in the air, as she rubbed his belly.

Ben nodded at her, his eyes briefly dipping to look down her shirt. "The bookcase is fun but not terribly clever for a place where you have a cleaning staff. If you worked at the hotel cleaning up and noticed that this one book was tipped over in the bookcase, what would you do?"

Melissa nodded along, shifting Bubbles, which dragged her V-neck shirt a bit lower. The smooth, creamy skin dipped down to an edging of black lace exposed above the top of her shirt. "I'd straighten that book. It annoys me in the picture."

"Exactly. Then the compartment pops up and you

know the secret. Then you tell the other staff members and they tell their friends. Basically anyone in town could know about the compartment, and who knows if there were guns in there at all." His eyes lingered on her cleavage until he caught me watching him.

Melissa sighed. "So we haven't narrowed down the suspects at all. The gun could have been in Carl's office, and he could have snuck in there, gotten the gun, and shot Stacey for some unknown reason. Or it could have been anyone in the hotel—"

"Or restaurant—there is a door from the office to the restaurant," Ben supplied.

"Okay, anyone from the hotel or restaurant or anyone that snuck in that knew about the guns in the bookcase or anyone who brought their own gun. Except me. I don't own a gun like that, and I certainly didn't know about the bookcase."

Magdalena nodded agreement. "Me neither."

"But it was such a great theory and explained why Heather is so hell-bent on convincing people that I did it." A small frown pulled Melissa's eyebrows together.

Ben was fighting the urge to stare at Melissa's breasts. I watched closely as his eyes were drawn down like magnets to where Melissa was fussing with Bubbles so she could pull up her shirt. Bubbles, in turn, was twitching and hooking a paw on the neckline then twisting to pull the shirt down farther. Ben stared, and his eyes were starting to widen in appreciation when I loudly cleared my throat. Magdalena and Melissa looked at me with confusion on their faces, but Ben knew exactly what I was doing. I shifted my weight toward Melissa. Ben and I exchanged a brief look, and he broke the stare first.

He checked his watch. "Is there anything else that you need to know? The store should already be closed."

I extended a hand. "Thanks, man, we're good."

We clasped hands, and I might have squeezed a bit too tightly, trying to crack his knuckles, before letting go.

MELISSA

Outside the gun store, Audio Jason helped remove and pack up our mics. Ryan was off to the side, clearly chewing out Rebecca. She alternated between mouthing back at him and looking away, embarrassed. I put Bubbles on the ground and snapped on a leash to allow him to water a daffodil on the grass. I wasn't quite ready to call it a night. I had barely seen Ryan at all.

"Hey, guys?" I waited until Ryan turned my way. "I really appreciate everyone working late and helping me talk to the gun guy. How about if I buy everyone drinks? There's this great little coffee house just a few miles away. They have this amazing alcoholic hot chocolate with kahlúa and vodka whipped cream. My treat."

Jason the camera man and Jason the audio tech immediately perked up and looked at Ryan.

He looked at me then back to the crew members, who were nodding enthusiastically. "It's not up to me. We are already running behind schedule so if they want to go back to the hotel—"

Camera Jason loaded his equipment into the truck. "Nope, I'm good for a drink."

Audio Jason put his equipment in as well and shut the back. "Me, too. Where we heading?"

I turned to Magdalena. "You in or out?"

She bounced into my shoulder. "All in. Are you thinking of the place a couple doors down from the Fish?"

I nodded then turned to Ryan. "The Fish is the movie theater that Priscilla owns. The place I'm thinking of is called the Tipsy Bean, and it's a few doors this side of the theater."

Ryan nodded. "Rebecca? Do you know where it is?"

"Of course. I'll meet you guys there."

We all turned to our separate cars to caravan over. On the drive, I had time to think about why I had offered to buy everyone drinks. I tried to convince myself that I was a good person who wanted to thank the crew who were working so hard, but my thoughts kept coming back to Ryan.

When he had stepped up next to me to quiz Ben about the guns and bookcase, I had lost all train of thought. When I scratched Bubbles in his arms, every moment of skin contact between us scorched my fingers. He was so hard to read, mysterious, and yet I had caught him looking at me. I wanted to talk to him for just a few more seconds, not on set while working, but casually.

As I passed the Tipsy Bean, I was surprised that there was no street parking on a Wednesday night. I turned right at the side street and pulled into a lot.

We assembled in a loose group and walked back up the block. I tried to maneuver near Ryan while wracking my brain for a way to engage in conversation, but the sidewalk was crowded with people milling about on the street with office trash cans full of popcorn, toilet paper rolls, and a variety of props.

I opened my mouth to ask Ryan if he had any hobbies, but he saved me the embarrassment of the corniest openers ever when he put a hand on my back and pushed me ahead of him to weave through the crowd.

As we passed the Fish, a sign in front of the theater declared it interactive movie night. The crowd thinned slightly as we passed, and the line in the Tipsy Bean was only a few people long. I thanked Ryan as he held open the door.

I tried to maneuver closer to Ryan while holding Bubbles off the ground, but the group kept shifting to let people pass by, and I needed to let the cashier know I would be paying for all the drinks.

As we waited for our order, I managed to catch Ryan's eye and smiled. He shifted around Rebecca, and I moved behind Maggie and had just opened my mouth when they called out my name to say that our order was ready.

I passed out the drinks then snuck a quick sip of my hot chocolate while Rebecca grabbed two tables outside. When I handed Ryan his drink, our fingers brushed against each other, sending chills down my spine. He escorted me to the front of the café and out to where the others had pulled together two small round tables. The two empty seats were on opposites sides of one of them.

I blew out a breath and squeezed between Rebecca and Maggie while Ryan took the other seat between the two Jasons. I took a sip of the alcoholic hot chocolate, normally a treat that sent me into instant bliss. It was still good but somehow lacking. I put the glass mug down and briefly caught Ryan's eye before he turned to ask one of the Jasons questions.

Rebecca and Maggie had started a conversation about dancing: ballroom, salsa, tango, swing, et cetera.

Maggie took a sip of her drink, cupping her fingers around the warm mug. "Do you dance, Mel?"

I scooted my chair forward a bit as people pushed past behind me, smacking me in the head with a grey trash can.

"A little. I took dance classes as a kid and did that thing where you learn how to waltz and put on your coat."

Maggie looked at me with one eyebrow raised, but Rebecca snapped her fingers. "I know what you mean. Cotillion. Hey, Ryan," she shouted. "Melissa did cotillion. Remember when we took it?"

Ryan laughed, his eyes scrunching up. "The lady that taught it had castanets and was always clapping them together to get our attention."

Rebecca put down her coffee with Irish cream, and I barely grabbed Bubbles before he sank headfirst into her mug.

Rebecca and Melissa started brainstorming about having the socialites go out dancing for the show. I wasn't particularly interested, so I turned my attention to the crowd at the theater, which was steadily growing. Besides the trash cans overflowing with popcorn, the crowd also shared the feature of wearing costumes, though there was no particular theme. Some were in steampunk gear of leather, lace, and goggles, while others were cosplaying their favorite anime or superhero characters. A few were in long gowns and tuxes.

I pulled my jacket closer around me in the chilly air and checked my phone for the time. I had an email from my agent titled "Immediate attention needed: Urgent." Apparently the reprieve was up, though I had no idea what I was going to tell her.

A gal bumped into me from behind, and popcorn rained over my head. I turned, and the woman—in six-inch wedge boots that reached her knees over fishnet stockings and a skirt that failed to cover her butt cheeks—was sitting on the back of my chair, the trash can of popcorn tipped backward over my shoulder. She smelled strongly of liquor and cheap perfume, the chemical notes biting my nose.

I took a sip of my mostly full drink and gritted my teeth. I lowered my voice to interrupt Maggie. "What is going on at the Fish? Who are these people?"

She rolled her eyes at the girl encroaching on my personal space and leaned in. "Interactive movie night. They play a popular or cult movie, and people come and interact. Each movie has a set of props people bring, and there's a guy that sells his stale popcorn by the bucketful. That's the big thing—they throw popcorn at the screen. I hear it's a huge mess to clean up, but apparently it's worth it."

A second shower of popcorn tumbled over my shoulder as the girl behind me brayed like a donkey. The popcorn wedged into my cleavage, and Bubbles snapped up a few pieces before I could wipe them away.

I took a deep breath, trying to let it go, but the gal adjusted her seat and pinched my hair in the process. I yelped as my head was yanked back. Then I was free and flew up out of the seat, holding Bubbles under one arm.

When I stood up, the chair flipped over backward, the girl landing hard on the sidewalk, her trash can tipping over and spilling on the ground.

She came up roaring. "What gives, lady?"

I jabbed a finger in her direction. "You sat on my hair. This is a single-occupancy chair. Where do you get off trying to sit in a chair I am already using?"

She picked up her trash can in horror. "You spilled my popcorn. You little—" She stopped with a gasp and stepped back. "You! You killed Stacey! Help! Murderer!"

People started turning around and milling behind her. Maggie grabbed my arm and turned to the group. "Time to go." She started pushing me toward the edge of the sidewalk, where the crowd was thinner. Ryan appeared at my other side and wrapped a protective arm around me.

Bubbles growled and barked at the girl, each high-pitched yip punctuated by a loud fart. The air around us grew stinky.

The girl blocked our way with a few friends and started throwing handfuls of popcorn. The gal grabbed a huge cup of water. "No one kills on my watch." She raised her arm to toss the drink in my face.

I flinched back, but right then a guy stepped backward between us, and the liquid intended for me splashed all down his side.

He roared around at the girl. "What gives?" he screamed and threw his drink in her face. What missed her hit a tall kid with a mohawk behind her.

In a flash, food and drinks soared in every direction. People started stampeding and chanting, "Food fight," over and over.

Cheers went up all around. I turned into Ryan's chest, and he wrapped two arms around me as he pushed me through the crowd.

"Ryan, my drink! No drink left behind." In the warmth of his embrace, the bizarreness of the situation was surreal.

I felt him chuckle. "It's too late."

I looked behind me, where popcorn was overflowing from my abandoned mug. The staff of the Tipsy Bean was pressed against the window, while the owner locked the door.

The rest of my group was hunched over, weaving through the crowd, with Ryan and me in back. Bubbles was still barking and wiggling to get free. I slowed to get a better grip on him.

The crowd surged and knocked me over. I twisted as I fell to protect Bubbles. My knees stung, and someone stepped back onto my hand. Bubbles was still barking in high-pitched, frightened yips.

Ryan shoved to shoo people away and scooped Bubbles out of my arms. "I got him. You okay?"

I nodded, trying not to cry. "I think so."

He grabbed my hand and pulled me behind him. We stayed in a low crouch as I followed him out of the crowd. Bubbles stopped barking, and I was safe in the space behind Ryan. Eventually the crowd thinned and we were able to jog back to the parking lot. Police tore up the street, sirens wailing, toward the theater.

Ryan squeezed my hand then dropped it as we turned the corner to the parking lot to join the rest of our group.

Maggie hugged me hard. "We were just heading back. That was crazy. You okay?"

I was still a bit mystified by the whole situation, how quickly things had escalated and the way that gal had gone after me.

Bubbles sat in Ryan's arms, panting with his tongue hanging out. "Let's all get out of here and go home."

Everyone went to their respective cars except Ryan, who opened my car door then passed me Bubbles once I was settled. "Drive safely, and don't think about what that chick said. She was drunk and looking for trouble."

I nodded, and he closed my door. I took a few moments to watch his backside walk away in the rearview mirror before heading home for bed.

CHAPTER ELEVEN

—————

Melissa

It was Thursday morning, and I should've gotten out of bed already, but Bubbles was sleeping on me. His nose was nestled next to my neck, and one paw was pressed against my nose. His breathing and occasional grunts of happiness had woken me up ten minutes ago, but I hadn't moved.

Instead, I thought about the show, the murder, and Ryan, not necessarily in that order. When I had told Ryan that I wanted to stay on the show to clear my name, I had meant it but hadn't given much thought to how I would do it. How do you prove you didn't do something? Perhaps you prove you were doing something else, but I couldn't prove I was sleeping. What I could do was prove that someone else had killed Stacey.

Why would someone want to kill her? That seemed like a good place to start. She had been annoying, but nothing I had seen was deathworthy. The first suspect was always the husband, though no one had seen him the day of the murder. I would have loved to pin it on Hateful Heather—she certainly had a vicious enough nature to kill Stacey.

Maybe they had disagreed on something, and Heather grabbed the hidden gun from the bookcase and shot Stacey. She dropped the gun and raced out, telling production that she had to take care of something and to put me into the room when I arrived. Then later she returned and pretended to be surprised when Stacey didn't appear. My gut said that her reaction had been real, but I was no expert on acting.

My intense dislike for Heather made this option, that she was the real killer, my favorite one so far.

Rebecca had told me about Heather's husband, Carl, being a playboy. Maybe he was having an affair with Stacey and Heather killed her in a fit of rage. Or Carl killed her so Heather didn't find out. Or Mike, Stacey's husband, killed her in a fit of rage. Too many fits of rage, and they all seemed equally plausible.

Repeatedly I'd heard that Mike was a bit shady. Ben, at the gun store, had told that story about Mike threatening to bury him in legal bills. And there was something about Priscilla going bankrupt and how it might be Mike's fault, though Rebecca didn't understand how it had happened.

The popcorn fight, while kinda funny in retrospect, had been scary in the moment. That girl had really seemed to think I was a killer.

The bedroom door opened, and my sister called out, "Uh, Meli, are you awake?"

"Yes, I'm awake. Bubbles is sleeping, and I didn't want to move."

Bubbles stirred and caught one of my nostrils with his claws, hooking and pulling it painfully. I gathered him in my arms and sat up.

Samantha was carrying the local newspaper. She sat on the corner of my bed nervously. "Amanda brought the paper with her this morning. I think you'll want to read the front-page story about the lead suspect in Stacey Rickman's murder." She handed me the paper.

Splashed across the front in bold letters was the title of the article, "Wanna-Be Writer or Accomplished Murderer?" I gasped. "What the fudgesicles? This can't be real." But it was. Under the fold was a picture of me on a gurney being rolled into the ambulance captioned, "Under the watchful eyes of the police, Melissa McBallister is wheeled away covered in blood."

I offered the paper back to Sam and buried my face in Bubbles's coat. "I can't read it. Just tell me how bad it is."

She sucked air through her teeth. "Pretty bad, M. The article paints you as a failed writer who saw the TV show as your last chance. You tried to kick Stacey off the show, and when it failed, you killed her."

I groaned.

"Mom's not going to be happy about this characterization: 'Melissa's mother, Mary McBallister, is best known as the literary heavyweight who wrote many bestsellers such as *Lost Widows*, but few know of her brushes with the law. Perhaps the criminal apple didn't fall far from the tree.'"

"No!" I fell over and pulled the comforter over my head.

It was no secret in my family that Mom had grown up in a rough neighborhood and gotten in trouble, but it was hardly the kind of thing that we bragged about.

The paper rustled again. "I don't understand this part about you starting a popcorn-fueled riot last night."

I shook my head. "Lies."

Bubbles was thrilled to go back to bed. He scratched at the comforter until I lifted the edge, and he crawled under to curl up along my side.

Through the comforter, I yelled back at Sam, "Bubbles and I live here now."

She batted at my feet. "Get out here. What are you going to do?"

"I don't know, Sammi." I pulled back the comforter and stared at the ceiling.

"I thought you were going to try to clear your name. If you want to do that on TV, you better get going."

"What do you mean?"

"The article says that a lobby of concerned citizens is trying to pressure the network to cut you from the show until the police charge you."

"They what?" I sat up and snatched the paper back to scan the article.

I gritted my teeth as I raced through the article, which described the first episode. It completely neglected any of what Heather had done or Stacey crashing uninvited but focused on what I had done, including references to my "mocking of dietary needs" and "ruthlessly forcing long-time local Stacey from the lunch."

I muttered to myself, "Who did Heather pay to write this article?"

Sam threw herself onto the bed and crawled up next to me. "Amanda told me that the reporter is good friends with Heather."

"That's not fair." I continued to scan. It ran through the details of the murder, stating that I was discovered by the body covered in blood, which was only partially accurate. I crumpled up the newspaper and threw it across the room.

"Mel, you need to clear your name. This isn't good for the resort."

I glared at her. "The resort? What about my reputation?"

"That, too. You need to get up and solve this murder. Do you know anyone that has some information on Stacey and who might have killed her?"

I snatched my phone off the nightstand and called Rebecca. She had promised to help me clear my name and get the information out to the general public.

She answered the phone. "Hey, Melissa, did you see the paper?"

"I did. That's why I'm calling. You know that gossip you told me about from the memorial service? The lady that told Ryan all about the rest of the ladies in the show. Can you set up a meeting with her? I have a few questions for her."

RYAN

One of the biggest pieces of advice I received about ensemble reality shows was not to get too close to the talent. Do your job, but stay distant. Your job is to create a compelling and interesting show, not to pick favorites. As Bubbles curled up in my lap in the back of the car as we took Melissa to meet Prudence Latrice Thursday afternoon, I knew that I was failing spectacularly. This was the opposite of staying distant and professional. I had an arm resting on the back of her seat in the crowded car. There was no way to avoid my hand resting on her shoulder, but I didn't even try to find a different way to sit. Her shoulder seemed so petite under my hand.

The morning had been a blur. Our unusual shooting schedule meant that several crew members had already taken off to pick up items from Cheyenne, Wyoming, a three-hour one-way drive. We had put another handful of crew members on a flight home to Los Angeles along with

Bobby when he took the footage to the editing studio. The illness that had decimated the crew had left a few people too weak to work. It made sense to send them home and try to find new crew instead.

Then Beth had raced into the production office that morning with the newspaper. The article about Melissa had been horribly one sided, but Rebecca was thrilled for the coverage. She assured me that this would blow over. When Melissa had called to ask about Prudence, Rebecca had used my guilt to convince me to call her and ask for a meeting.

I had been so sure that Prudence would refuse that I didn't give it a second thought. I had mentioned that Melissa wanted to meet with her and that I assumed she was much too busy. I had given ample opportunities for her to back out, but Prudence, much like every other woman in my life right now, had surprised me. She'd insisted we come over immediately and bring the cameras.

I tried to explain that cameras weren't necessary, but she had read the article and had some things she wanted to share with the world. Rebecca had snatched the phone from my hand and used her considerable charm to thank Prudence for her honesty and bravery, and yes, of course, we needed to do whatever possible to right the wrong against Melissa. They set up plans for an afternoon tea, and directions were given.

I had sat with my head in my hands and wondered when this production had gone off the rails. I had a standing Thursday-morning call with Ian, though the last meeting had been cut short, as he had his own reality show to worry about. Apparently teaching reality stars to dance was going to be almost as difficult as keeping socialites from dying. I had broached the topic of the extra footage of Melissa investigating who killed Stacey. I'd hoped he would tell me that it was an awful idea and as executive producer, he was putting his foot down. Instead he had told me that it sounded like a good idea, and he was pleased with our numbers. I had free rein to do as I pleased, but he had to go talk about tangos, tap dancing, and dance studios.

I could've put my foot down and said no. But when I followed up with Melissa, her voice had been full of tears until I said that Prudence would meet with her. Then her voice bloomed up with hope and thankfulness. I thought about the food fight the night before and how her voice had still been thin and weak when she asked for a time and place to meet us. Before I knew it, I'd offered to pick her up and told her that Prudence insisted that she bring Bubbles.

She had thanked me profusely. Her shaky voice had told me she still felt weak after yesterday. I had insisted it was no bother and to take her time. I'd felt protective and accommodating. A few hours later, I was bouncing around next to her, with Bubbles crawling all over my lap.

"Bubbles likes you," she said.

I was startled out of my thoughts and looked at the tiny dog curled up in my lap, licking his business. I jiggled my leg, and he stopped to stare at me. "Bubs knows I'm alpha around here. Dogs respect that."

"Bubs?"

"No self-respecting dog wants to be called Bubbles. We have an understanding."

She smiled at me in the closeness of the car. She was wedged between me and Audio Jason. He had volunteered to work today, not only to pick up a few extra bucks, but he was curious to see what was said. The crew was placing side bets on who'd killed Stacey, and many of them had more than a passing interest in clearing Melissa's name. At least I wasn't the only one whose professional detachment was shattered.

Rebecca was driving while Beth gave directions to a quiet and expensive neighborhood on the far side of the river on the mountain facing the ski slopes. The houses were large, secluded, and stately. They carried the old and heavy mantle of money and respect. Rebecca was a careless driver and was hitting the corners a bit too fast. Melissa paled a bit after a dodgy corner.

I cupped her shoulder with a soothing squeeze. "Rebecca, take it easy."

Melissa rested her head on my shoulder and squeezed her eyes closed. "Give me just a second."

"Sorry, I'll slow down." Rebecca pressed hard on the brakes.

Melissa lurched forward then covered her mouth.

Jason leaned away and into the window. He had one hand on the door handle, ready to leap. His side of the car clung to an edge of road the dropped steeply down into the river below. Jason grimaced and looked between Melissa and certain death.

We pulled into the driveway and parked. I got out of the car, holding Bubs under one arm, and grabbed Melissa's arm to help her out. When she stood up, I stroked her back. "Are you feeling okay?"

She smiled at me, her face regaining color slowly. "Yes, the fresh air's helping."

Jason got her mic pack on, and they went inside. A nice brunette in sensible pants welcomed them in.

She introduced herself as Maria, and I asked her to pass on to Prudence that we would be outside. Melissa was feeling a bit sick.

"She caught that bug that is going around town. She

needs to eat more garlic." The not-altogether-unpleasant scent of garlic wafted off her hands as she gestured to the house. It was a dark wood house with beautiful stained-glass windows. It wasn't as large as the sprawling homes in the newer area of town, but the details were immaculate.

Bubs squirmed in my arm, and I passed him over to Melissa. I realized I was still stroking her back and let my arm fall to my side.

She pulled a leash out of her pocket and clipped it on Bubs's leash before putting him on the ground to explore. He danced and picked his way through the dirt as though he was trying to avoid getting his paws dirty.

"What's Prudence like?"

"You might call her Mrs. Latrice. She's a force to be reckoned with: a bit cranky and quick to snap but funny."

"You say that like it's a compliment." She lazily walked around the front yard.

"Women worth loving aren't easy," I said paraphrasing my grandmother.

"Then you must be crazy about me." She laughed.

"I am." It slipped out between us casually and nestled in the space between. It was truer than I cared to realize.

She stopped and looked at me.

The front door slammed open, and Rebecca stormed out the door. "We've got a problem."

CHAPTER TWELVE

MELISSA

Ryan turned to his sister as she exited Mrs. Latrice's house, but I continued to watch him, trying to determine what he'd meant. If someone else had said they were crazy about me, I would have said they were hitting on me, but then it would have been accompanied by a cheeky wink or a peek down my shirt. Ryan had said it as fact. Maybe he just meant that I was a good cast member. The electricity between us might have been all on my side. He certainly didn't look as bothered as I felt when he walked over to his sister.

"What's up, Bec?"

"Prudence, or Mrs. Latrice as she is now insisting I call her, will only sign the filming release if you join Melissa at tea. She says she only agreed to meet with Melissa because she assumed you would be joining her."

"Okay, I'll join them."

"The producer can't be in the scene."

He shrugged. "I told you we're not using this footage."

"Fine, whatever. Just get miked and we'll settle this

later. Maybe we can just use the footage of Melissa and Mrs. Latrice. Thank goodness I brought the second camera for me to use."

Ryan unbuttoned his shirt, and Jason attached the microphone to his broad chest. I looked away as the heat rose in my cheeks.

Amanda had said Prudence Latrice was from an old family in the community, which seemed to be a quality of great importance. Additionally, she was old money, the two features combined to mean that she knew all the gossip, both recent and long forgotten. She had a reputation as difficult and cranky but also was known as a champion of fairness and abhorred even a whiff of corruption. Amanda felt that Prudence would be the best person to help me.

Not that I needed help, Amanda had been quick to clarify, but she avoided my eyes, and her voice was a little too shrill as she repeated that everything would be fine. Then she had remembered a task in her office that she had to deal with right that second.

"Hey, Mel. You ready?" Ryan called over as he buttoned his shirt.

I took a deep breath and nodded.

"Sorry, is it cool if I call you Mel? I don't know where that came from." He held open the front door for me as I passed through. His woodsy scent caught the edges of my awareness.

"Mel's fine. You probably heard my sister or parents call me that."

"You seem nervous." He squeezed my shoulder then patted me on the back, sending chills down my spine.

"A little." I stepped away from him and his distractions. Though I felt more confident as we followed Rebecca down a hallway, I had to drag my mind away from thoughts of Ryan. I could worry about that another time.

Rebecca signaled to us to stop. "Sorry, but we're short-handed. Wait to enter until about ten seconds after I call to you."

Ryan fidgeted next to me and muttered to himself. "They don't teach you this in film school."

I giggled and warmed in the private moment. "They need to update the curriculum to include what to do when your cast member is accused of murder." Bubbles squirmed in my arm, and I shifted him to the side closer to Ryan.

"How to solve a murder on set." He smiled at me.

"Killing the competition." Bubbles extended his paw toward Ryan and whimpered. The traitorous dog.

Rebecca signaled us to enter in ten seconds.

Ryan leaned over. "What I really needed to learn was how to stay off camera when your sister is the director and forces you into the middle of this mess. Ready?"

I nodded and counted to ten before entering a formal room ahead of Ryan. It reminded me of what I had imagined a parlor would look like. There were large windows with a view of the ski slopes across the river on the other side of the valley. There were still patches of snow stubbornly clinging in mounds, but much of the mountains held a tint of bright green where the grass was poking up through the mud.

The room had one large chair upholstered in a pink rose pattern across from a wide loveseat. Between them was a table with a teapot and matching tiny plates in a rose pattern similar to that on the chair. The room was small but felt cozy rather than cramped. Bookcases lined every wall. The smell of old books mixed with the scent of tea. There was a bench under the window, and I could imagine sitting there, reading and watching the weather go by.

"What a gorgeous room." I spun around again to take it all in, my eyes skipping over Beth and Rebecca as they filmed and Jason crouched outside the door recording audio. I realized I hadn't even greeted Prudence Latrice, who sat in the upholstered rose chair. "Pardon me, Mrs. Latrice. I'm Melissa McBallister. Thank you for meeting with me." I caught myself curtsying like a time-traveling debutante instead of an accused murderer. I swayed slightly during the unfamiliar gesture as if I was slightly drunk. When had I ever curtsied in my life?

She dipped her head once then turned her attention to Ryan. "So glad you could come." She put a hand on the arm of the chair as though she was about to rise.

Ryan walked over. "Please stay seated." He scooped up her hand and squeezed her fingers then leaned over and gave her a kiss on the cheek. "I eagerly jumped at the chance to see you again."

She smiled at him, and the color in her face brightened. "Oh, you." She lowered her eyes and batted her lashes at him as he squeezed her hand again.

For a split second, I could see the young woman she must have once been and, in a way, still was. She had not outgrown the desire to flirt with a handsome man or be complimented, and Ryan had seen that. He seemed genuinely fond of her as he smiled at her.

She reluctantly drew her hand back then seemed to remember me standing there. "Please, have a seat." She gestured to the loveseat.

I sat down nearest the window and placed Bubbles next to me in the middle of the seat. Ryan joined us.

"You like my room, Melissa?"

I stopped fussing with Bubbles, who wanted to sniff everything over rather than sit down and behave. "Yes, Mrs. Latrice, I love it. Whoever decorated it has quite an eye. It feels rich and comfortable at the same time."

"Thank you." She leaned back in her chair and smoothed out her pants. "I decorated it myself. And please, call me Prudence. The only people that call me Mrs. Latrice are my banker and service people. Maria!"

A middle-aged woman swept into the room with a silver tray. "No need for caterwauling. I'm right here. I've brought the—Bubbles!" She stopped dead in her tracks.

Bubbles yipped and barked, dancing on his tiptoes.

I set Bubbles on the floor, and he raced over to the woman to scratch at her leg.

She placed the tray on the low bookshelf near the door and swept him off the ground. She rocked him in her arms, where he licked her nose and face.

Prudence turned in her chair. "How do you know Bubbles?"

"He belonged to my previous employer, but I thought he went to the family." She set him back on the floor, where he ran in circles around her feet.

I leaned forward. "He was in the shelter, and I adopted him."

Prudence crossed her arms under her massive bosom. "If you had just watched *Savvy Socialites of Fishcreek Falls*, you would have known."

"Reality television will rot your brain," said Maria. She looked at Ryan and me. "No offense intended. Let me show you a trick that Bubbles and I used to do. Sit." She stepped back as Bubbles sat, a skill I hadn't realized he performed on command. She pointed her index finger at him with her thumb straight up in an imitation of a gun. "Stick 'em up."

Bubbles sat up on his back legs, his front paws reaching toward the ceiling.

"Bang!" She pulled her hand up as though the imaginary gun had been shot.

Bubbled yipped as he ran in a circle once then collapsed on his side.

I laughed and clapped. "Bravo. I'd no idea he knew any tricks."

He was perfectly still until Maria spoke again. "Okay."

He jumped up, and she scratched behind his ears. "Go sit. I'll get you a treat in a bit." She turned around and grabbed the silver tray. "I didn't realize he was in the shelter. Poor little guy, but he looks good now." She came over and used long tongs to move bakery items onto our small floral plates.

She placed a long, glazed twist in front of me. The doughnut lay diagonally across the plate and hung off the scalloped edge at one side. Then she placed two cupcakes at the other end, one on either side of the twist.

I stared down at the white icing–covered treat.

She continued to pass out the confections, leaving me gaping at the rather obscene display.

I glanced at Ryan to see if he noticed the similarities, but he was already biting into the twist. Prudence, on the other hand, had a hand to her chest as she gazed at her plate. "Reminds me of my dear Albert."

Ryan choked on his doughnut.

I slapped his back until he was able to catch his breath, then I turned to Prudence. "Good memories?"

She gave me a quick wink then poured some of the fragrant coffee into Ryan's cup. "Drink up."

Ryan gulped down his drink then slid the doughnut

back onto the plate. He'd bitten on the top. "Prudence, I hope you don't mind if we get down to why we came."

"Let's. As soon as I read the paper this morning, I made the decision that if you asked, I would tell the whole story. When you called, it seemed like a sign."

Maria had left the room and returned with a plate of cut-up carrots that she placed on the chair next to Bubbles. He leaped on them, grabbed a carrot, and chewed loudly while little flecks of orange sprinkled around him. He let a little fart slip as he munched.

I picked up the crumbs and put them back on his plate before adding a bit of milk to my coffee then to Ryan's when he lifted it in my direction. "I read the article as well. Very upsetting. I hope you know that the allegations are untrue."

"Of course they're untrue, but that doesn't mean they can't hurt you just the same. Heather and her husband are shysters."

Maria shook her head. "Not shysters, Prudence, anything but shysters."

"Don't you tease me. It's true. As crooked as a dog's hind leg and twice as muddy. Carl Beckett and Stacey Rickman, God rest her soul, were having an affair. Probably why Stacey put up with Heather bossing her around. Guilt."

Maria put her fists on her hips. "Don't say such things unless you saw it with your own eyes."

Prudence stared back at her defiantly. "If I saw that with my own eyes, I'd have to gouge them out. Now get out of here. We have gossip to share, and you're far too pious to hear such things. Go on."

Maria shook her head and muttered under her breath as she left the room. "Stubborn ol' goat, why I oughta..."

I called after her. "Thank you for the food, Maria."

Prudence turned to us by way of explanation. "She is a

wonderful nurse and like a daughter to me. But she doesn't like me gossiping. She worries about my immortal soul, but God made me this way and should have given me a bit more discretion. Besides, it's not gossip if it keeps you out of the electric chair."

I swallowed hard. I had no idea if the electric chair was still in use or what Colorado's stance was on the death penalty. Regardless, it was true that I had been accused of a horrible crime—if not by the police then by the public, who could be twice as brutal. There was no parole from the punishment of a small community that thought someone was guilty. No judge, no jury, no attorneys could clear your name.

I cleared my head and throat with a quick cough. Those things could be worried about later. "Are you sure about the affair between them?"

She nodded. "Definitely. My sister Chastity—you met her, Ryan—her housecleaners have a niece that works at the hotel and walked in on them in the very office that Stacey was killed in."

I gasped. "No."

"Yes."

Drifting in from the hallway came Maria's voice. "Don't trust gossip. You know how people like to tell stories."

Prudence dismissed the thought with a wave of the hand. "Go on, Maria. No eavesdropping from the hallway."

She shook her head at us and continued. "I'm sure the story is true, but it wouldn't hurt for you to meet with her in person. Her name is Linda Brown, and she just started working at the Bunny Ear Hotel."

"I thought you said she worked at the Trumpett Hotel." I picked off a corner from the cupcake. My stomach was still dodgy, but the red velvet cupcake with cream cheese frosting was too much to turn down. The tanginess of the frosting offset the sweetness of the fluffy cake. I licked my fingers quickly then wiped them on my napkin.

Ryan watched me, and Prudence nodded in approval. "Good cupcakes, aren't they? I'm telling you, Ryan, make sure you marry a girl that appreciates good food. You can only spend so much time in bed."

I snorted, but when Ryan's jaw fell open, I howled with laughter. He looked like a fish as his mouth moved to speak but nothing came out. "Remind me not to get into a war of words with Prudence."

Ryan looked at me. "She's not wrong."

I looked down at the cupcake to hide my flushed face.

Prudence laughed in her seat. "Oh, I see. Interesting."

I avoided her eyes as heat rose in my cheeks. She was blunt enough to point out whatever weirdness lay between Ryan and me.

Bubbles was no longer interested in the empty plate but instead had his nose raised. He sniffed around and edged toward Ryan, who held his coffee cup in his hand and rested it on his knee. Bubbles stalked toward the coffee until I swept him up and placed him on my far side, away from the temptation.

Prudence leaned back in her seat and ran a hand over her necklace, adjusting the clasp to the back. "Melissa, you have been nothing like I expected."

"Oh? How so?" I wasn't sure where she was going with this, but as long as we got off the topic of food and bedroom activities, it would be a blessing.

"I've read all your mother's books, did you know that? Of course you don't, I just told you. They're beautiful, serious, deep, and tackle big issues. I met her a few years ago, I think it was a charity event for literacy, and I found her to be much like her books: beautiful, deep, and serious. When I read in the paper that you were going to be on the show and they said that you were also a writer and you described your writing as a modern day literature, like your mother, I assumed you would, in fact, act like your mother."

This topic was no better than the last. She wasn't the first person to tell me this, and I prepared to defend my work. A frustration built up inside of me like a match bursting into life. It flared fast and hot. A writer didn't need to be a certain way in order to write that way. I'd started to speak when Prudence stopped me.

"Hold on, let me explain. Nothing I'm saying is an insult. I think you're smart and very witty, especially on the show, and the world needs more of that. Your mother's work is brilliant, but it is also very sad. Moving but difficult. I don't see that in you. You have this quick tongue and a mind that skips along. Why don't you write like that?"

I had a catalogue of fast, easy answers and grabbed one. "I want to deal with important things and move people in a—"

"I don't need one of your pageant answers. I lost a child, and when I was grieving, it wasn't deep books or important things that helped me most. It was Lucille Ball, Carol Burnett, Erma Bombeck, and the like. It was laughing until I cried tears of joy rather than loss. It was the reminders of all that is light and good in the world. People *need* humor." A tear rolled down her cheek, and she dabbed it away with a lace hankie. "Now enough of that. What were we talking about?"

It took me a second to catch my breath after her admission. "You were saying that Linda no longer works at the Trumpett Hotel?"

"She used to work at the Trumpett but switched to the

Bunny Ear Hotel. I think her family insisted she change jobs after the murder. The local hotels are always terribly understaffed. People come to ski but think they're too good to actually have to work for a living." She shook her head at the state of such people.

"Thank you. I'll stop by and double-check with her. Assuming that Carl Beckett and Stacey Rickman *were* having an affair, what does that mean? Could Carl have killed her to keep it a secret? Did Heather know?"

"I believe Heather and Carl have an understanding of sorts, which I have never understood. Why would you want to share the person that you have pledged your life to? My dear Albert never gave another woman a second glance in all the years we were together. That was the greatest gift he could give me. Remember that, Melissa: a wandering eye on a husband is worse than teats on a bull."

"Yes, ma'am, I wouldn't imagine putting up with that. My father sounds a lot like your Albert. I bet Albert worshipped the ground you walked on."

Prudence nodded and gazed out the large window. "He did, the fool." She said it kindly and quietly, more to herself than to us.

I wondered if I would ever love someone as much as she'd loved her dear Albert. "Thank you for sharing about the affair. That's pretty big news." I broke off another piece of cupcake to shove into my mouth.

"That's not even the big news. I gave it a lot of thought and wanted to tell you about Mike Rickman, Stacey's husband. I told Ryan that I felt that Mike was a crooked lawyer, and I want to explain why I said that." She took a deep breath and let it out but didn't continue.

I looked at Ryan, who raised his eyebrows, then I turned back to Prudence while the silence stretched out. I dissected the second cupcake, pulling off the remaining wrapper and carefully pulling off a piece that had the perfect cake-to-frosting ratio. I didn't need to eat anymore, but it was calling to me. Foul cupcake temptress. "If you don't want to say, I totally under—"

"No, I need to share this. I've given it a lot of thought." She nodded decisively. "When I say Mike is crooked, I mean it. Albert's brother Henry was on the city council, and he had a problem with liquor. The family did their best to hide it. He never drove drunk. Not once. There was a big vote coming up for rezoning, and if the vote went one way, Mike's client would benefit greatly. This was back when Mike first moved back to town after getting his law degree. Henry was one of the swing votes, and..."

My stomach flipped as I saw where the story was going.

Prudence stared out the window again before continuing the story in a rush. "Henry came to Albert and said that if he didn't vote for the rezoning, word would get out about his drinking. At that point he was drinking seven nights a week, and it was starting earlier and earlier in the day. He was known as a conservative family man with a business-friendly platform and a hard stance on drugs. He felt he was backed into a corner. Albert told him that the best approach was to handle it head-on." She shook her head and looked at her hands, the weight of all the years rolling over her again.

Ryan nodded along. "Albert was a smart man. It's not the crime that gets you, it's the cover-up. What did Henry do?"

Ryan's words seemed to bolster her. "Henry checked himself into rehab that day. He was so embarrassed, but the town rallied behind him. Overall, it was the best thing that could have happened to him. The weight of the secrets had been crushing him. After he returned, he started speaking with at-risk youth, and overall he was a bit gentler. I think the entire experience made him a better person. More understanding."

"Blackmail. How terrible." I rested my chin in my palm to think. If Mike was blackmailing people, that opened up a lot of new possibilities. Had Stacey known? Was she also blackmailing people? "How did Mike find out about the drinking? Was it common knowledge?"

"No." Prudence shook her head adamantly. "It was after his divorce when he was back living with my mother-in-law, God rest her soul. Her long-time maid had left town right before it happened, and we always wondered if she had said something. She was the only person that wasn't family who could have known, because Mrs. Latrice was so careful. Since I talked to Ryan at the memorial service, I've been thinking about things a lot, and I'm sure that is what happened with the Trumpett Hotel deal and Priscilla."

I looked at Ryan. "Trumpett Hotel?" This was all new to me.

Ryan's delicate coffee cup looked like a toy in his massive hands. He put it down and shrugged. "I don't know."

I turned back to Prudence. "The hotel that Heather and Carl Beckett own and where Stacey was killed. What does that have to do with Priscilla?"

"Let me start from the beginning. You know that Priscilla and Richard Morrison are property managers, right?"

I nodded.

"They were developing a little strip mall next to the hotel and were in the process of buying the hotel. Everyone in town thought the deal was done because they had signed a contract and placed a down payment. The whole deal depended on getting the hotel, and things were rolling along when suddenly they pulled out, and Heather and Carl bought the hotel at a much lower price even though they had been outbid by Priscilla and her husband initially. Priscilla and Richard lost the down payment, and because of how the deal was set up, they had to abandon the whole project with the mall, which put them into bankruptcy. They eventually got everything paid off, but it was a tough decade for them."

"Why would they back out of the deal and go bankrupt? I assume this is related to Mike Rickman?"

She pointed at me. "Bingo. You are a smart girl, aren't you? Yes, Mike was involved. I haven't given it any thought in years, but after talking to Ryan, it really bothered me. The deal with the hotel, I mean. I lay in bed all night and talked to some friends the next day. I'm very confident that I have what happened worked out."

She held up a hand. "Before I tell you, I want you to know that I'm only telling you this because the risk of hurting anyone innocent is long gone. I wouldn't repeat this story if it was still a secret." With finality she let out a deep breath.

I nodded. "I understand."

"Priscilla got pregnant in high school and married Richard. They had a daughter, and for whatever reason, she was wilder than a stallion. They did their best, but Bethenny, that's her name, was a holy terror. She was boy crazy and maybe a little crazy in general, skipping class, partying with football players, drinking. You get the idea. Right around the time of the hotel deal, Bethenny was in Europe, *studying abroad*." Prudence put extra emphasis on the last two words, trying to convey a meaning I didn't understand.

I wanted to connect the dots that she was laying out for me. She had just told the story about Henry going to rehab, so maybe they were connected. "Bethenny wasn't studying abroad, was she?"

Prudence shook her head. "No. We knew she was wild and politely believed the lie, never asking for too many details. These are the types of things you do for other families: you nod and believe them when they tell outrageous lies. But when Heather accused you of murder, I was willing to dredge up the truth. I don't feel badly about sharing it because Bethenny has been clean for a decade."

That answered the question of what she had been hiding. "Drugs?"

"Yes, Bethenny had gone from partying to a full-on drug addiction. She spent time in rehab and outpatient treatment along with therapy. Since then she's gotten married, had two beautiful children, and started a charity for young adults who need rehab but can't afford it. Nowadays she is very open about the whole story, but when she was seventeen, her family would have done anything to protect her."

"Priscilla and her husband went bankrupt to protect her. How heartbreaking."

Prudence caught my eyes. "And someone had threatened them. Either let the whole town know that their underage daughter was addicted to drugs or give up the hotel."

I pushed the plate of cupcakes away from me. "That's sickening. Then Heather and Carl Rickman bought the hotel?"

"Yes." Prudence nodded and looked out the window, where the dark-grey clouds had let loose a spring storm.

Rivers of water rained down from the edge of the roof. "I don't know how much they knew, but they'd used Mike as a lawyer since the moment they moved to town. They may be awful people but I don't think they're stupid. They know."

One time could be a coincidence, but now it was starting to sound like a plan, a strategy. "Are these the only two times that you've heard of, Prudence?"

She shrugged. "Yes and no. I've seen some things that make me suspicious but nothing else that I can prove. A deal that was a little too good to Mike's client. I'd assumed that he was a very good negotiator because I never gave it much thought. But once I thought about Henry... Well... now I'm not so sure. Please, know that I never would have brought Bethenny up except that she is very open about her story and past drug abuse. Nothing I said today about her drug addiction is a secret now. I just put the pieces of the puzzle together to see how it connects to the hotel business. I wish I could tell you who killed Stacey. She certainly didn't deserve to be shot like a dog in the street."

CHAPTER THIRTEEN

Ryan

Wedged into the backseat of the car as we left Prudence's house, I was uneasy. No, freaked out was a better description. Learning that Carl was blackmailing people was a new angle that made the whole situation more serious.

I had my arm resting on the back of the seat, my hand brushing Melissa's arm, and I resisted the urge to draw her into my chest and protect her. Rebecca as well, though I felt a bit guilty that I hadn't thought of her first, being my sister and all. It probably was just because, as production, Rebecca was safer and hadn't been accused of murder. That must have been it.

Melissa sat in the middle of the backseat and chewed on her thumbnail. She hadn't spoken since we got into the car after talking with Prudence. She was lost in thought, far away. My hand squeezed her shoulder before I could stop myself. She leaned into me but didn't pull out of whatever thoughts she was having.

Jason was playing on his phone as always, tapping away

like a woodpecker. Rebecca and Beth were chatting in the front seat about directions. I squeezed Melissa's shoulder even harder. "Hey, what's going on inside that head of yours?"

She looked at me with wide eyes. "What? Oh." She sighed. "We went from no suspects to too many. I'm trying to work it all out."

"Tell me."

"Priscilla and her husband had a reason to be angry with Mike if he had blackmailed them, but why wait so long, and why wait until we were about to film? But if Mike did that to Priscilla, and we know he did it to Henry Latrice, then who else was holding a grudge? And why Stacey? Why wasn't Mike killed instead? The timing bothers me a lot."

The words tumbled out of her mouth like a waterfall. I was only half listening, instead enjoying the melody of her voice. "Why?"

"Why wait until national attention was on Stacey? If they had killed her a month or a year ago, it wouldn't have been on national television. My sister texted me—Stacey's murder is on all the major networks."

"Crime of passion? Coincidence?"

She shook her head and tapped her nail on her front teeth. "My gut says the timing is related to the murder. The murder happened the morning after the show premiered, so maybe there was something on the first episode that set someone off. Or the fact that she was on the show at all. She wasn't even supposed to be on the show, right?"

I chuckled. "She was supposed to be on the show, but Mike was such an awful negotiator that..." I trailed off, and the other shoe dropped.

"Mike was a bad negotiator? The same guy that

Prudence said always got his way and blackmailed people into deals that benefitted his clients?"

A sick feeling rolled through me as the obviousness of the situation hit me. I hadn't given Mike's negotiation tactics a second thought, having been more than happy to assume he was an idiot. "That jackwagon."

She turned in her seat, her knees nudging up against my legs. "Tell me about what happened."

I scrubbed my hands across my face, frustrated with all the obvious signs I had missed. "I gave them a standard contract. It was slightly in our favor but definitely nothing crazy, but he kept coming back with revisions. Each time they were more outrageous until I finally cut Stacey loose." I shook my head. "I figured he was a lousy negotiator and had overplayed his hand. But now…"

"You think he did it on purpose?"

I ran through my interaction with Mike. The surprise when I'd given in to Stacey's request for Wednesday off, or the right to be first in the show intro. The time he even suggested in an email that maybe Stacey wasn't the best fit. "He's not an entertainment attorney, so I figured it was a case of him being out of his depth, but he could have done it on purpose to have me cut her." I pulled my hand into a fist.

"It's okay. You had no reason to suspect him, and even if you had, you still would have cut her. But why did he want her off the show?"

Her legs pressing up against me were a distraction. I struggled to focus on her words between the heat of her body pressed up against me and the delicate whiffs I caught of her soap, perfume, or something. "No idea."

The car lurched as we pulled into a driveway of a hotel in town. Not our hotel but the Bunny Ear Hotel. "Becca, what's going on?" I asked though I knew already.

She called over her shoulder. "It was on the way. I figured Melissa could run in and ask Linda Brown about the rumor. It would only take a second."

"We're not filming it." I turned to Melissa. "You don't have to do this if you don't want to."

She shook her head. "No, this is perfect."

Becca parked then looked at us. "We'll wait here. Take your time." She sat back in her seat.

I caught her eyes in the rearview mirror and narrowed my eyes suspiciously. I would find out what she was up to later. "I'm going with Melissa." I stepped out of the car and offered a hand to Melissa.

"You don't need to go in—" she started.

"I want to stretch my legs." I had no idea why I was making excuses rather than just saying that I wanted to protect her. As a producer, it would be totally normal to try to protect the show and the most popular cast member. The two most popular cast members if you counted Bubs cradled in her arms.

I opened the door to the lobby, where a lady lazily talked on a cell phone with her feet on the counter. I approached the desk. "Is Linda Brown working today?"

"Hold on," she said into her phone around the smacking of her gum. "Yeah, she's cleaning rooms on the second floor. The elevators are around the corner." She dove back into her conversation, spinning her back to us as she whispered into her phone.

I stepped around the corner. After pushing the button, we stepped into the waiting elevator. "Do you know how you'll handle this?"

"Are you offering to be bad cop to my good cop? Perhaps threaten to rough her up if she doesn't spill the beans?" She giggled at her own joke and bounced into my shoulder playfully as we entered the elevator.

I debated laughing against telling her to be careful until the doors dinged open and she took off in search of Linda.

I blew out a breath holding all the things I'd left unsaid and followed as she skipped down the hallway to a cart in front of an open door.

She popped into the room, and her voice trailed behind her. "Hi. Are you Linda?"

The other end of the conversation was lost until I caught up. I was debating hanging back in the hallway until the elevator dinged with another load of guests. I ducked into the room and found Melissa talking to a young brunette who was making up a bed.

The brunette cast suspicious glances at Melissa while stuffing huge pillows into cases. "I need to finish this room." She looked at Melissa then did a double take before gasping. "You're from that show, the sassy ladies show? Heather says that you killed Stacey." She covered her mouth with a hand and stepped away.

Melissa's face fell. "I didn't kill anyone. I was hoping you could help me. Prudence Latrice sent us over."

Emotions raced over Linda's face before she continued. "Mrs. Latrice is a nice lady. She's paying for my brother to go to medical school." She focused on the last pillow, and when she was done, she looked to Melissa. "You're her friend?"

"Yes. Prudence knows I'm innocent and thought you could tell me about Carl Beckett and Stacey Rickman having an affair?" Melissa stated it as a question and waited for confirmation.

Linda let out a sigh and turned to me. "Can you close that door?"

I clicked the door shut and joined them at a table set near the window.

"Yes, Carl and Stacey were having an affair. I was double-checking one of the empty rooms at the Trumpett and walked in on them a month ago. He was a dog."

Melissa turned to me. "Carl could have killed Stacey to keep Heather from knowing. Or maybe Mike Rickman killed his wife to cover up the affair."

Linda shook her head. "It couldn't have been Carl."

Melissa leaned forward. "Why? How do you know?"

Linda looked away before standing up to tidy the night-stand, straightening an already perfectly situated lamp.

"What is it, Linda? Please," Melissa begged.

Linda slumped over and flopped onto the edge of the bed. "He was hitting on me during the time of the murder. I feel so stupid. I thought he was interviewing me to be a manager. Since they, I mean you, were filming in his office, he said he would conduct the interview in the penthouse suite. I was dressed in my best outfit, and right when I saw him"—she pointed at me—"we went up to start the interview. We didn't leave until Heather called his cell phone like five times to find him. By the time we came downstairs, the police were already there. But nothing happened between us despite his best attempts. He was working up to it, I could tell. Talking about the importance of working as a team and understanding each other. He kept touching my arm."

Melissa curled her top lip back. "Ew, gross. What a sleazebag."

Linda nodded at Melissa, the two caught in a moment. "Yes, exactly, a sleazebag. My parents wanted me to quit because of the murder. I agreed, but mostly because I wanted to get away from Carl. Everyone knew he was grabby, and I didn't want to fight it anymore. But he didn't tell Heather about it. He said that our meeting only lasted ten minutes then I left. Clearly he felt pretty guilty about having me in the penthouse so long."

Melissa got out of her seat and sat on the bed next to Linda. "Did you tell the police?"

"Yes. It was very embarrassing. I don't think they believed that we were just talking. They probably thought I was trying to sleep my way to the top."

"Hey, I believe you. Did you see Heather that day? Could she have done it?"

Linda pursed her lips and looked at the ceiling. "Maybe? I don't know. She was yelling at everyone to clean up, that the TV show would be here soon and not to ruin it for her. I went outside before anything happened. Sandra, a coworker, said that there was a problem with the washers, and Heather tore her up one side and down the other. They had used the wrong soap, and there was water and suds everywhere. I'm pretty sure Heather couldn't have killed Stacey. I mean, maybe, but Sandra said she had to talk to the police like forever, explaining where she was and for how long."

Melissa nodded along. "Anything else that might help me?"

Linda shook her head, her brown ponytail whipping her face. "No."

Melissa stood up to leave then paused for a second before continuing. "I can't promise anything, but our family is opening a resort in the fall, and I might be able to get you an interview if you want."

"Are you for real? I'd love that." Linda sat up straight, her bangs falling across her right eye until she swept them behind her ear.

Melissa held her hands up. "I can't promise anything. The interviews will be open to everyone, but I can make sure they know that you helped me. And if I can remember, I can message you. Why don't we exchange phone numbers?" She pulled out her phone and poked at the screen like an expert.

Carl was a sleaze but not the murderer, and it sounded like Heather could be in the clear, but none of this helped Melissa clear her name.

They'd finished exchanging numbers and were hugging.

Melissa checked her phone. "We'd better get going."

As I headed to the door, I heard footsteps in the hall and held up a hand to warn Melissa. We waited until the elevator doors clanked shut to step into the hallway.

MELISSA

Sitting in the car after leaving the Bunny Ear Hotel, I absently stroked Bubbles's fur as he lay in my lap. I was jammed between Jason—the one that did sound, not Camera Jason—and Ryan. I had learned a lot but was no closer to actually clearing my name. When we pulled into another hotel, I looked around.

Rebecca pulled to the front entrance and left the car running. "Thanks so much for filming today. Why don't you guys call it a day, and I'll run Melissa home?"

Jason and Beth hopped out of the car, and I took Beth's seat up front.

I was buckling up while Ryan leaned through Rebecca's window. "You're taking her right home. No investigating. I know you both"—he made eye contact with me—"think this is some game. Someone killed Stacey."

Rebecca rolled her eyes at her brother. "I'm not a kid."

"Exactly. That's why you have no excuse to behave like an idiot."

"Hey!"

He looked at me again before shaking his head and turning to Rebecca. "I don't trust the two of you together. Straight home then come back, no stops."

She blew out a breath. "Fine. That is what I was planning on doing anyways. Bye." She rolled up the window, cutting off his reply, and slowly pulled away. "Brothers." She looked at me and rolled her eyes. "Is yours like that?"

"No. He's the middle kid between Samantha and me, so he's more like the peacekeeper or referee. But Sam's bossy, too. Probably an oldest-child thing. Ryan is the oldest, right?"

She checked both ways before pulling out of the parking lot. "Yes, it's just the two of us. How are you feeling?"

"Not great, not awful. I'm tired but way better than I was yesterday. I would feel so much better if they caught the killer and I could put that behind me." I sighed.

"I wanted to talk to you about that, but can we keep this between us?"

"Breaking big brother's no-investigation rule, are you?"

She shrugged. "Not really. I mean yes, I think we should keep investigating, but it's not like we'll do anything dangerous, and that's really the spirit of what he was saying."

I chuckled and recognized the little-sister sneakiness in her answer. "There is something in this that I'm missing. Besides the killer, I mean."

"Tell me what you know. We can brainstorm the next step."

I wasn't alone in wanting to clear my name, and it bolstered my spirits. I sorted through the facts and decided to list what we knew chronologically. "Mike Rickman, Stacey's husband, is a lawyer and a crook. We know that he tried to blackmail Henry Latrice, and we think he blackmailed Priscilla and her husband, Richard Morrison. He may have blackmailed others. But what does that mean? Priscilla's situation was more than a decade ago. Is she still mad? Why be on the show if she was mad enough to kill Stacey? She did sign up at the same time that Stacey did, right?"

"Yes. Priscilla didn't really say much about anyone, but she knew the others cast on the show and didn't make a peep. Do you think Stacey knew what was happening?"

I'd had only a few passing experiences with Stacey. She had been whiny and meek. In the episode I had seen, she'd burst into tears. "Maybe. It wouldn't be unusual for a wife to know her husband's dealings. But... Hold on."

Something was bugging me. I shuffled through the conversations that I'd had with Prudence and Linda from the hotel, but instinctively I knew that wasn't what I was looking for. The only other place I'd talked was in the car. That was it. "Ryan brought up the bit about Mike negotiating Stacey out of her contract. If he was honest with her, he would have just told her not to do the show. There were secrets between them."

"The affair between Carl Beckett and Stacey? The blackmailing that Mike was using in his practice?"

"Either? Both? I'm not sure, but he didn't want her on the show. I feel like her murder is connected to the show."

"Really? Why?" She whipped around a corner.

I grabbed my seat belt to steady myself and put a hand on Bubbles to keep him on my lap. "Gut instinct, I guess.

Either someone was scared something would come out, or something did come out and we missed it. Maybe I should watch the episode again."

What if someone had seen something in the episode that made them decide to kill Stacey? What would it have been? "She was killed the morning after the episode aired. I wish Heather and Carl Beckett didn't have alibis. They would be perfect suspects."

"Probably why Heather was so eager to point the finger at you."

I nodded. "Maybe I should find out what Priscilla was up to."

"I'll do that for you, if you want. Tomorrow and Saturday, I need to work all day on next week's production schedule and a few others things. I could poke around Barbie's and Priscilla's alibis."

"Thanks, Rebecca. That'd be great." We were approaching the edge of town.

"What do you want me to find out?"

"Just find out what Priscilla and Barbie were up to, just in case. I'm pretty sure that Mike is the key. If Mike is corrupt, why did Stacey die?"

We waited at a red light, and she turned to me. "If you want to brainstorm more, why don't I come over Sunday? I can tell you what I found, and we can watch the show again and talk?"

"I'd love that." I smiled back at her.

"I'm sure you'll be super busy until then." She laughed.

I looked at her in confusion. "Doing what?"

"Writing? I mean, that's why you got on the show to begin with, right? I bet you have so many ideas right now."

I hadn't given a single thought to writing, but she was so

excited for me that I played along. "Totally. Get my mind off things. Turn right here."

She cruised where I pointed.

"They say to write drunk and edit sober, so I'm going to need more vodka. There's a liquor store."

Rebecca pulled into a spot in front of the liquor store and started to unbuckle.

I handed her Bubbles. "Stay here. I'll only be a second." I flew out the door before she could protest and pushed into the store.

I meandered back to the vodka aisle, an area I knew well, though I was a little less enthusiastic about my purchase this time. Having to wait until Sunday to continue our investigation seemed like far too long.

I grabbed a serviceable vodka off a low shelf, and when I stood up, an old man stood blocking my path. He had a long white beard and wrinkles deeply etched into his rough skin. He was far closer to me than was comfortable, and he was staring.

I jumped back in surprise, clutching the bottle to my chest.

He stepped closer, blocking me into a corner. "You're that girl that shot that lady on TV."

My mouth hung open, and I was starting to protest when he cut me off. "People have been known to take justice into their own hands."

My hands trembled on the vodka, and I pushed back into the wall.

"Bill, leave that girl alone and let the police handle it," the owner of the store called from the end of the aisle. He made eye contact with me and glared. "You take that vodka and get out of here."

I ducked around the man when he turned to face the

owner. I caught a whiff of tobacco and smoke and raced to the door, throwing a twenty on the counter, more than enough to cover the vodka.

I pushed the door open and flew into the car, barely closing the door before yelling at Rebecca. "Drive. Go!"

With a raised eyebrow, she passed me Bubbles and pulled out of the shopping center and onto the road out of town. "What's wrong?"

My fingers trembled as I stroked Bubbles's back. "There was this guy and..." He hadn't said much. I thought he was threatening me, but maybe I was overreacting. I swallowed hard and slowed my breathing. I didn't want to sound ridiculous. "He was just kind of creepy."

She snuck a few more glances at me, and I summoned up a weak smile.

She narrowed her eyes. "Your face is really white."

I pressed a hand to my face. "I'm just tired. Really. What were we talking about?"

She pulled onto the dirt road, the last stretch until we reached the ranch. The fields on either side were no longer just brown and muddy; now green blades pushed up through the dark soil. Spring always felt so hopeful, a fresh start. I was on a television show, had adopted a dog, and was having more fun than I'd had in years. If it hadn't been for the pesky murder accusation, I'd have been all set.

She shook her head. "What will you write about?"

I stared out the window. "Oh, I don't know. I have a few projects in the works." They were terrible, but I could keep that part to myself.

"Can I ask you something?"

"Sure."

"I thought the same thing as Prudence, I mean the part about you writing funny books rather than serious books.

You know that I love your mom's books, but I think I would love books with your sense of humor as well. The blog you wrote last week about the show was hilarious. Everyone loved it, especially me. Have you ever written a comedy or something humorous?"

She had no idea what a loaded question that was. I thought of the secret emails from my agent. No one knew about those projects. They had started on a lark, but they were getting under my skin. It was an issue I had been ignoring for a while. And suddenly everyone wanted to talk about what genre I was writing in. I would have loved to talk to someone about it, but Rebecca might be tempted to use it to her benefit to promote the show. I was still debating what to say as the moments stretched on.

She parked the car in front of the house and turned to face me. "I didn't offend you did I? I'm just being selfish. I think you're hilarious and would love to read a book like that. I didn't mean anyth—"

"No, you're fine." I got out of the car, grabbing Bubbles and the bottle of vodka. "Call me when you're up Sunday. Bye."

CHAPTER FOURTEEN

MELISSA

Long ago, I had fallen into the habit of writing in sprints. I would set an alarm for thirty to forty minutes and write until it went off. Then I would spend a few minutes stretching and moving in general while thinking of the next section. Sometimes I was so engrossed that I turned off the alarm and kept writing until I ran out of words. Other times I would take a short walk to figure out what to say next. If I was blocked, I might spend the time writing about my day or a cat, anything just to get words down on the page.

Thursday night I had not slept well, tossing and turning with nightmares until sunrise. I grabbed a few hours of sleep then groggily got up to try and work. I had napped on and off most of Friday between work sessions, but no actual work had been accomplished. I had checked the news stories, forums, blogs, et cetera. I'd decided to write back to my agent a soon as I accomplished some work, but I hadn't written a word. That was fine. I hadn't had a day off in a while, but Saturday I set the goals of really getting back to work.

I had gotten up that Saturday morning, eaten, and taken care of Bubbles then sat down to work precisely at nine a.m. It was now four p.m., and I had barely half a page of words. I had been staring at them for so long that they no longer made sense. If I was honest, I knew they hadn't made any sense when I wrote them.

My head was full of laughter and adventure, murder and intrigue, a small dog that was a professional actor and a screeching lady who accused me of murder, along with cameras, mics, and televisions shows. All the excitement and activity had made my world bright, loud, and colorful. Sitting alone in my room trying to write felt dull and grey in comparison.

I had poured myself a glass of orange juice and vodka this morning, but it still sat untouched on the corner of the desk. A fly did lazy backstrokes on the surface. I groaned, took the glass to the bathroom, and poured the whole mess down the sink. I didn't feel like drinking anyway.

This wasn't the first time that I'd had trouble writing, but this time it felt different. It wasn't uncommon for me to struggle with how to express an idea, but this was troubling. Since I had been old enough to walk, I'd wanted to write like my mom, and I was no closer to that goal than I had been when I was four. It had been my dream, my goal, and my identity. What would it mean to lose that? Who would I be?

I had found an old outline for a short story, and I tried to work on it, but getting words out felt like pushing ketchup through a colander. Some days were like that. After several hours of torture, I had made myself a light lunch to take back to my bedroom. What Prudence and Rebecca had said was digging into me. In between bouts of pecking at my keyboard, I would find any excuse to stop work. This meant a full-body massage for Bubbles, playing with toys, and practicing his tricks. Despite my personal angst, Bubbles was having a great day.

After giving Bubbles a bubble bath, I opened up a blank file to start my show blog.

Suddenly the words were flowing faster than I could type. It was fun and easy and felt right. The comparison between what I had struggled with all morning and the ease of this project scared me. I edited it and chuckled as I read over my thoughts and feelings about being accused of murder and my determination to clear my name and sent it off to Beth for posting after the show aired.

I turned back to my first project, and my chest constricted with anxiety. Instead of writing, I spent the next two hours staring out the window while a spring storm tore through the valley, and I finally came to the decision to talk to my mom.

People were always surprised when I said that my mother and I didn't talk about writing. My college peers had imagined that we gathered around the fireplace in the evenings to discuss the craft of literature, but that had never been the case. She went into her office, closed the door, and worked. When she left the office, she left her book in there, both physically and mentally.

That was how it had always been in the McBallister family.

My email dinged. There was another email from my agent with the subject line, "Is there a ghost of a chance for us to talk?" I really needed to reply... later. I closed my laptop with a click and called Bubbles to my side. Interrupting Mom when she was writing was a banishable offense on the ranch, but this was an emergency. I was mid-existential crisis, and that wasn't even taking into account the murder accusation. The lawyer wasn't concerned since the police hadn't even bothered with a follow-up interview, but his neck wasn't on the line, was it?

I dragged myself down the hallway to Mom's office, where I knocked and waited for her voice to answer before pushing the door open.

"Hey, Mom, I'm really sorry to interrupt but... can I talk to you?"

She closed her tablet and set it on the desk. "Sure, sit down." She gestured to two chairs.

Her office was what I imagined the ideal writer's studio to look like. Dark wood bookcases lined three of the walls from floor to ceiling. For years, they had stood half empty with figurines and plants filling the empty space, but once my parents had moved here, the knickknacks had been removed to house her impressive book collection. In the center of the ceiling was a low-profile but impressive chandelier that bounced light around the room.

The two chairs had backs that rose above my head when I stood next to them. The backs and seats were embroidered in the style of medieval tapestries. One displayed a hunt scene of a deer being shot with an arrow, while the other had a pack of hounds attacking a fox; both were gruesome. My mother sat in the other chair, transferring her mug of coffee onto the table between us. I took a deep breath as the anxiety welled in my chest again. Mom was a smart and accomplished writer. Surely she could help me.

I sat down and slapped my leg until Bubbles jumped up. He sniffed air until his eyes rested on the mug of coffee. My feet dangled off the ground, and the chair's arms were set so wide that I couldn't rest my arms on them, increasing the sensation of being a small child looking for Mom to make it all better.

"Do you ever feel like you're writing the wrong thing? Is that just a normal part of writing?" I began.

She leaned back in her chair, showing no emotion on her face. "How so?"

I fidgeted, scooting forward until my toes grazed the carpeting, then picked at some lint on my pants. Maybe this had been a bad idea. "I don't know... I just thought... I just need to write and not worry." I put a hand on an armrest.

"Melissa, don't go." Mom took in a deep breath then let it out slowly. "You know that I try to respect your journey and path, but I've been wondering about you for a while." She stared out the window.

I waited for her to continue, knowing that long pauses were a sign of her internal thought process. Unlike dad, who was a talker, she was a thinker. Bubbles stepped onto the armrest and leaned toward the table, sniffing frantically. I scooped him up and put him on the far side of the chair, where he glared and farted in defiance.

Mom wrinkled her nose. "How is Bubbles doing?"

"Wonderful. The vet said that some dogs are gassy. We made some changes to his diet." Bubbles crawled into my lap and farted again when he sat. "They aren't working."

My mother smiled then cupped her chin in her palm and pursed her lips. "Is this conversation about the memoirs?"

I shrugged; I wasn't sure what this was about exactly. I had written a few memoirs in conjunction with the people who had lived them. They were important stories that the world needed to know, but they weren't my stories.

"You are doing great work with the memoirs, and if that's what you want to do for a living, then that is fine." She watched my face closely.

"I like them, but they aren't... my calling? I feel like that is work I do to give back rather than my purpose." I struggled to put my thoughts into words. She was my mother, but we never talked about this type of thing, and I felt vulnerable.

"What does excite you? What is your passion?"

"Literature, deep, meaningful stories that make people think." This was an answer I had known my entire life, and I was able to reply without thinking.

She shook her head. "No. I know that you say that, but stop and think. When you think about these deep and meaningful stories, do you really feel joy?"

"Of course I do." I crossed my arms and huffed. I didn't even want to question this part. I had come to her for a solution to my writer's block.

She held up her hand. "Let me change tack for a minute, if I may. You know that Grandma and Grandpa didn't have a lot of money growing up, and we lived in a very poor area. Plus I didn't always make the best choices. I learned early on about poverty, discrimination, and the will to overcome. That drove me to share my stories with the world. After I was married and had you and your sister, I learned about a mother's love, and I wanted to share that with the world. When we lost Grandma, I wrote about a motherless daughter. Do you see what I am saying?"

I shook my head and guessed, "You shared with the world what you knew?"

"Yes, but I wasn't born with that, it was the result of my life, what I experienced. My regrets, my pain, my loss, my joy. I had to experience life first. You have always been so smart, so cautious. You learned from all our mistakes and avoided your own."

"So I need to go screw up?"

My mother's clear laugh cut the air. "In a way, yes, go

have big adventures, big loves, big losses. You have holed up in this house all winter, hiding from the world. The more you hide, the less you will have to say."

I kicked at the carpeting. "That's not what happened to Emerson."

"You, my dear, are in a different boat than Ralph Waldo Emerson. Consider this a writing assignment. I want you to go live big. Say yes to everything. You have said no for far too long."

I gave her comment some thought. "I don't always say no. I joined the television show."

She tapped her chin, her eyes laughing. "Exactly."

I waited for her to explain more, but that seemed to be the sum of her point. In frustration, I blurted out, "What's that supposed to mean?"

"I read your blog about the show. It was very good."

"Thank you. It was just something that I threw together."

"No, Melissa, it was more than that. It had more of your personality in it than anything else you have written that I've read. How do I say this?" She clasped her hands together with index fingers pointed up. She tapped them together as she thought.

I petted Bubbles, both eager to hear her thoughts and nervously dreading her insight. The moments stretched out forever.

"I was very much against the reality show because it would have been an awful decision for me and my career. But for you... You are becoming more you. I think you are on a different path than me."

"But I've always wanted to be a writer!"

"And you can be, but there are a lot of different topics in the world. I think you need to spend time thinking about what kind of writing will make you happy long term. What excites you? What were you made to write?"

I groaned in my chair. Frustration constricted my throat. "Can't you just tell me what to write?"

"If I could, I would, sweetie, but that is not how this works. I can't tell you the answer to that, but I can pray for you and listen if you want to talk. That's about it. You are the *only* one that can answer this question."

MELISSA

Sunday morning, Bubbles stretched across my throat as I stared at the ceiling, questioning every assumption I'd ever had about myself. We had gotten up, had our morning constitutional, and crawled back into bed. I was having a small emotional breakdown, but Bubbles was enjoying the extra bed time while we waited for Rebecca to call.

What made me happy? People spent a lifetime trying to figure that out, and yet didn't everyone know instinctively? I knew that I liked to make people laugh, I loved my dog, and I was discovering that I loved adventure. I'd thought I loved great literature and deep thoughts, but I couldn't remember the last time I had yearned to delve into those topics.

I was not sleeping, but I didn't feel fully awake either. My mind danced from topic to topic. I had made the mistake of scrolling around the Internet, where I discovered that Stacey's murder and Heather's accusations were headline news everywhere. I'd thought the story was big a few days ago, but now it was international news. My inbox was full of emails from people I hadn't spoken to in years. My agent had sent another email with the subject line, "We're not breaking up, are we?" I had turned off my computer, determined to deal with everything tomorrow.

The only one I replied to was the editor of my secret project. She had suggested that we shelve it until my schedule opened up. And when it did, she had some ideas for us to chat about. How had my life gotten so complicated?

When my cell phone rang, I was thrilled to see Rebecca's name pop up on the screen. I answered the call with, "You ready to come over?"

Her voice chuckled on the other end of the line. "I forgot to call before I left. I'm in your driveway."

"Oh crap!" I shifted Bubbles onto the comforter then ran into the closet to grab clothing. "I'll be down in a second."

I raced down the stairs and let her in. I waved to my family as they left for church, which I was skipping to try to clear my name. I was sure God would understand.

I ushered Rebecca in. "You can come up to my room while I get ready. What did you find out?"

"Barbie and Priscilla were together. Can you believe that? They were with their husbands at the River Side Café during the murder. The café offered them a free brunch the day after the episode aired. They wanted to cash in on the show for tourists. The café was pushing the idea that people wanted to come by and eat because they might run into a reality star."

I set Bubbles back down on the bed, where he scratched at the blanket across its foot until it was formed into a nest. Then he curled into the middle. I pulled up a corner of the blanket to cover everything but his head.

"They were there the whole time. Are you sure? It would be convenient, but how do you know?" I went into the bathroom to apply a few swipes of basic makeup. When we'd filmed, I had done the full makeup that felt like applying paint to the side of a house, coat after coat of expensive product. It was not my style at all.

"They both claimed they were, but I figured we could double-check. I made us a reservation for a late brunch–early lunch thingy in two hours. We can poke around."

"Smart." I ran a brush through my hair, debating what to do with it. Maybe a French braid?

"They were totally booked up until I mentioned you and Bubbles wanted a patio table. Then they couldn't make room fast enough."

I poked my head out of the bathroom. "Seriously? You name-dropped *me*, and it worked?"

"Totally. And I talked to Magdalena, even though you didn't ask about her. She was with her brother in Denver picking up supplies for the store."

I checked the braid in the mirror then wrapped a soft fabric elastic around the braid at the base of my neck, leaving the rest of the hair to hang free but out of my face. "Maggie's not a suspect. Get real." I left the bathroom and started to rummage through my walk-in closet for a jacket and boots to complete the outfit I was already wearing of slim, stretchy pants and a loose-fitting top.

"You need to be objective if you are going to solve the murder and save the show."

"The police need to be objective. I don't. I can focus on my gut and keen attention to detail. Speaking of which, did you just say 'Save the show'?"

"You know that they were only going to do four episodes? With Stacey's murder being discovered on air, we're not sure what'll happen. On one hand, the free publicity is out of control, and you are all over the news.

They're predicting tonight's episode's rating will be crazy high."

I grabbed my knee-high boots with a low heel in green suede and sat at my desk to zip them up. "That's great."

"Yes, it's great, but there is also a push to get you, the murder suspect, and the entire show off the air. They're having a network meeting Monday morning to talk about it. But if you can prove you're not the murderer and we can get it all on camera, can you imagine it? You'd be a hero, and they would for sure pick up the rest of the season."

"You're telling me that your offer to help me clear my name wasn't just to help me? You had ulterior motives?" I laid enough sarcasm into my words that she had to know I was kidding.

She laughed. "Hey, we have the same goal. If we catch the killer, clear your name, and save the show, then we can live happily ever after. All your dreams will come true."

Sounded good except that I needed to figure out what my dreams were. "Do we have time to watch the first *Savvy Socialites* episode again before we leave?" The network had it loaded up on the website, and I had figured out how to watch it on the television.

"Totally, but what are you looking for?"

I stood up, unwrapped Bubbles from his blanket cocoon, grabbed the jacket, and headed downstairs with Rebecca trailing me. "Not sure. Possibly nothing, but keep an eye on Stacey, just in case. Do you want a bottle of water or anything?"

"Sure. I can grab one if you tell me where they are and get you one as well."

"Thanks. The TV's in here. The kitchen is down this hallway, at the end on the right. Water's in the fridge." I pointed down the hall before ducking into the room where they had filmed my discussion with Maggie. I fiddled with the television until I had the episode loaded up.

Rebecca tossed me a bottle of water as she joined me and settled into the couch to pet Bubbles.

I started the episode and cringed. "It is so weird to watch myself. It makes me really self-conscious."

"Don't worry. A ton of people feel that way, even actors."

The show played on as thoughts churned in my head. When I had seen this episode the first time, I had still been very sick, and much of it was a blur. When we had filmed, I had been painfully aware of the cameras for the first five or ten minutes, but after that, I had forgotten they were there.

Priscilla's talking-head interview, the one in which it was just her looking at the camera and talking about her life, was playing. I studied it for some glimmer of information.

Rebecca turned to me suddenly. "Get this. I talked to Heather about filming tomorrow and casually asked about the murder. Once she was done fuming about you being the killer, she claimed that she was with her husband Carl during the murder."

I chuckled. "Do you believe her or Linda?"

"Linda, totally. Heather was super defensive about it."

I'd started to turn my attention back to the show when a thought occurred to me. "What are we filming this week?"

"Beth's sending out the final confirmations tomorrow, but Tuesday, Barbie is having a dermatology party at her husband's office; you can buy fillers and Botox at a discount."

"How modern and vain. I love it."

"Wednesday, Magdalena is having a demonstration at the family's hot shop, and we'll finally finish the interviews for the week's episode."

Bubbles rolled onto his back, and I took the opportunity to scratch his belly. "No filming on Monday?"

Rebecca let out a sigh. "Not for you. Heather is holding a breakfast at her restaurant, and she only invited the other girls."

"Oh, for goodness' sake." I rolled my eyes.

Rebecca held up her hands. "I know, I know. I told her that she was acting like a high schooler on national TV but that it was up to her."

"I don't know what high school you went to, but I was never accused of murder at mine. This is a whole new level of crazy."

Rebecca chuckled. "If you want to plan your own event for Tuesday, that's up to you. Call Beth tomorrow to make the arrangements."

I nodded and settled in to focus on the show as best I could. Conflict and drama between people was often referred to as being "high school behavior," but was that really fair? I hadn't seen any difference between conflicts in high school and college or any of the conflicts I'd experienced in elementary or junior high for that matter. There was this cultural expectation that adults behaved differently, perhaps more maturely, but I hadn't seen any evidence of that. Fighting was fighting, and age didn't seem to affect the quality or quantity of it.

With the exception of family stuff, when was the last time I'd had conflict with someone? I must have gotten deeply lost in my thoughts, because I was startled when Rebecca spoke up.

"Are you watching this at all?"

"Totally." The show was already at the restaurant fight scene. "This is hilarious. Watch as Malcolm comes over to the table then veers away because of Heather."

I was surprised, though: Malcolm veered away before Heather even started speaking. I grabbed the remote to rewind it. "That's not how I remembered it. I thought that Heather drove him away."

We watched it again, and I let it keep playing. "That's so weird. It looks like he turns away when he sees Stacey."

Rebecca was deep in thought. "Did you hear what Stacey started to say to him? She recognized him but seemed surprised that he was there. Let's ask about that as well when we're at brunch. Have you heard anything more from him?"

"Nope. Typical of my dating life." The more I thought about it, the more frustrated I got. He wasn't all that interesting. I should've been the one to blow him off, not the reverse. "You know what? Can we come back after brunch and watch this from the beginning? I'm starving, plus I need to get out for a bit."

Rebecca stood up. "Sounds good to me. Grab Bubbles and we'll go."

CHAPTER FIFTEEN

MELISSA

When we arrived at the River Side Café, there was quite a crowd of people waiting in bunches outside. We were early, and I expected a long wait as well, so I loitered on the sidewalk. I pushed Bubbles into my ski jacket to keep his furless belly warm. He scanned the crowd through squinty eyes, probably looking for a mark to give him a treat.

Rebecca went in to check on our reservation, and when she came back out, she called me over. "Melissa, our table's ready."

I self-consciously wove through the crowd to the front door as people stared, probably angry that we had a table or that I was holding a dog at a restaurant. I didn't even want to think about someone else accusing me of being a murderer. The hostess, rather than escorting us through the café, walked us down the sidewalk to a small gate that led to the patio area. It was chilly, but gas heaters were set up to keep diners warm outside.

I felt guilty about going in when everyone else was

waiting and jumped when a lady stepped in front of me. I braced myself for an angry confrontation.

"Excuse me. You're Melissa McBallister, and this is Bubbles, isn't it?"

I searched my memory but didn't recognize her. "Uh, yes."

She squealed and called back to her friends. "I told you. We *love* you and the show. So you really eat here? That's so cool. We decided to eat here but had no idea we would actually see you. We're such big fans. Can we get a picture? Please?"

I was at a total loss for words, but Rebecca came to my rescue. "Melissa would love it. Here, I'll take the picture." She held out her hand for the cell phone the lady had pulled out. "Melissa, make sure I can see Bubbles."

The ladies gathered on both side of me.

Rebecca held up the phone. "Say 'socialite' on three. One. Two. Socialite."

We all chanted 'socialite' on cue, then they excitedly shook my hand.

Rebecca grabbed my elbow and started to drag me away. "Enjoy your meals, ladies, and thank you for watching the show."

People were pointing and snapping photos as we followed the hostess to the table.

I was in total awe. "Wow, I can't believe they wanted a picture with me." I sat at the table and adjusted the chair to make sure Bubbles had an adequate amount of heat from the gas heater.

The hostess handed us our menus. "Are you serious? This is the best week we've ever had during mud season. Everyone wants to check out the café—locals and tourists."

She turned to me. "You actually being here will be a real benefit to us. Thank you so much."

I wasn't sure how to respond. "You're welcome?"

The hostess smiled and left.

Rebecca was smirking. "Your first time?"

I picked up the menu to check out the fare. "First what?"

"Meeting fans."

"It's a pleasant surprise after all the accusations. She wanted a picture with me." I shook my head and perused the menu before settling on eggs Benedict.

A waitress approached the table. "Hello, Melissa, Rebecca. I'm Meg, and I'll be your server today."

I looked up at the waitress who already knew my name and recognized her as the waitress that Heather had snapped at when we filmed. "I'm so glad to see you. I wanted to apologize for the way the lunch went. I was horrified."

She waved a hand at me. "Not your fault at all. I saw the episode. Thank you for leaving a tip. You didn't need to do that, but we appreciated it. You know we are all Team Melissa."

"Oh?" I looked at Rebecca, who shrugged, then back to Meg.

"Absolutely. No one here believes Heather that you killed Stacey. You can trust a good tipper. We tell everyone that asks—and a lot of people have asked—that we know that you didn't kill Stacey. I even told Barbie, Priscilla, and their husbands that when the news came in about the murder. We knew from the second it happened that you were innocent."

"They were here when you heard about Stacey's death?"

She nodded at me. "Yes. They had been here for a few hours. We told them to stay as long as they wanted. People were already starting to show up that morning because of the show's premiere the night before. They were so excited to see cast members. Another one of the waitresses had signed up to be notified if the show had any live footage— great idea by the way—and saw the video then showed the rest of the staff. I was the one to show it to Barbie and Priscilla. They thought it was a publicity stunt, but Mikey the cook texted his cousin at the police station and confirmed that it was real. So crazy, a murder in our little town."

Alibis confirmed, and we didn't even need to nose around much. I shook my head in sympathy. "I'm still in shock. It doesn't seem real, but the newspaper article made me realize some people are taking the accusations seriously. That's upsetting."

Meg looked over her shoulder then kneeled down and lowered her voice. "Natasha's here."

I lowered my voice to match hers. "Who's Natasha?"

"Natasha Gruntal. She's in the corner table with red hair and a purple blouse. She's the reporter that wrote that article."

I sat up and scanned the interior dining room. At a corner table, a redhead in a purple blouse was already staring at me. When our eyes locked, she stood up, threw down her napkin, and stomped toward us.

I held Bubbles and stood up. The metal chair I had been sitting in screeched on the paver stones of the patio. There were two other tables on the patio, and the occupants turned around to watch.

Natasha pushed open the patio door and pointed at me. "How dare you?!"

I reared back in shock that was quickly replaced by red-hot anger. It constricted my throat, and my vision narrowed down to just her. "How dare me? I'm innocent. How dare *you* write such an accusatory and inflammatory article? You twisted every fact to fit your agenda."

People all over the restaurant were turning to watch. The ladies we had met earlier were leaning out the door taking videos.

She put her hands on her hips. "I got those facts from a reliable source."

"If you mean Heather Beckett, then you should know that she's biased. Only a hack would publish gossip as fact."

"I'm no hack. Why you little—" She was stepping toward me with her hands raised when suddenly she lurched back, her words cut off.

A woman had her by the back of the blouse. "Natasha, you need to leave. I won't have you attacking *my* guests in my restaurant."

Natasha turned, her face falling. "Penelope, you can't kick me out."

"I can and I will. I read that article as well. I know that you and Heather are friends, but you should have known better. Now leave."

Natasha threw a glare over her shoulder then pushed the video-recording lady out of the way and signaled to her fellow diner to leave.

I had huddled over to protect Bubbles when I thought Natasha was going to attack me, but now I stood up straight again. "I'm so embarrassed for that scene." I cringed to see the fellow diners gawking. "Let me pay for their meals. I sincerely apologize."

Penelope gave me a once-over then snorted. "That crap that Natasha tried to pass off as news was bound to get her in trouble eventually. That being said, I'm sure that your fellow diners would appreciate you paying for their meal. Excuse me while I check on them."

I slunk back into my seat, cheeks aflame. The silence that had fallen when everyone was watching the confrontation was replaced by the din when every conversation restarted at once. Bubbles crawled onto my chest to lick my cheeks. I rubbed a napkin across them to remove dog spittle but felt comforted by the gesture.

Meg, the waitress, inched back to the table. "I'm sorry. I didn't realize she would go after you like that. And don't mind Penelope. She's a grump at the best of times, but her son ran off this week."

What were the chances that two guys ran off in the same week? "Is her son Malcolm?"

She nodded. "That's him. He was supposed to be training to take over the restaurant, but he was never around. He had 'important work' to do." She did little air quotes with her fingers. "He was never around, so I don't care if he left, but it's weird that he ran off to a monastery. He wasn't even Catholic."

"He wasn't?"

"His family's Lutheran. No monastery would want him anyway. He's one crooked snake in the grass. I don't know what he was up to, but he had all this creepy stuff in his car like binoculars, tape recorders, video cameras, and such. But I can't get caught talking about the boss's son. Have you decided what you want to drink?"

"Orange juice for me." I turned to Rebecca.

"Me as well." After Meg left, Rebecca turned to me. "How are you feeling?"

"I think I'm getting used to crazy people trying to accost me." I contemplated the information about Malcolm. "I think we should try to find out why Malcolm ran off right after the murder. Do you think there are many monasteries around?"

"You said that he sent you a picture? Send it to me. I think Beth can pull the geotag off of it."

I pulled out my phone and tapped around until the picture was sent to Rebecca's phone. "How do geotags work?"

Her phone dinged. She typed out a message and put it back down. "It might not work, depending on his phone settings, but there's a chance that when he took the picture, GPS coordinates were attached to the photo. Beth's awesome at all that. I told her what we are looking to find out. What are you thinking?"

"Hadn't given him much thought, but it's weird that he ran off when he did. Then Stacy's reaction to him in the show combined with Meg's comment about his secret important job and a bunch of spy equipment... I think he's connected with Mike Rickman's blackmailing scheme."

Rebecca rubbed her hands together. "Oh, that's a good point. But how does that relate to the murder?"

"I don't know. That's why we need to find him."

Rebecca's phone dinged, and she bent over to read it. "We're in luck. Beth got us the info and says it's a few hours away in Wyoming. Want to head up there after brunch?"

"Sounds like a plan."

MELISSA

"Melissa, lazybones, we're here."

I sat up with a snort and caught Bubbles as he started to

slide off my lap onto the floor of Rebecca's car. "Did I fall asleep? I was supposed to be navigating."

Rebecca chuckled. "Your phone gave me the directions I needed. Technology, eh?" She turned the car into a gravel driveway that led to a bumpy parking lot.

I remembered entering the address that Beth had sent us. It was to a Catholic retreat center. I had turned on my navigation app and reclined my seat a little to get comfortable. That was the last thing I remembered besides a bizarre dream I'd had about a giant eggplant with red hair chasing me around Fishcreek Falls, threatening to send me to jail.

Rebecca parked and turned off the car. "I didn't have the heart to wake you. Ryan went back to bed this morning. He has the same illness you did, and he's still dragging."

I flipped down the visor and swiped mascara smudges from underneath my eyes. "I didn't think I was tired, but I guess I was." I dug a leash out of my purse and snapped it onto Bubbles's collar. I put him onto the ground outside the car to take care of business and followed him out to a bush. I stretched my arms over my head in the sparse, dappled late-afternoon sunshine cutting through the trees.

Rebecca bent over to touch her toes. "Man, I'm stiff. The ride back tonight is going to be rough. We're not going to get back to Fishcreek Falls until late tonight. I'm going to call Ryan and let him know that we went on an adventure, but I'm not telling him why." She chuckled as she dialed her phone.

I did the same, letting my sister know so she wouldn't worry. I wandered the parking lot while Rebecca continued to talk about production details that couldn't wait until she returned.

It was time to formulate a plan of attack. Once we found Malcolm, was it better to ask him to confirm what we suspected, that he was spying on people for Mike, or say that we already had proof? And really, I had no idea how this whole thing tied in to the murder. What if he was the murderer? I swallowed hard at the thought.

Rebecca clicked off her phone and joined me. "Ready?"

"We have to stick together. We don't know how Malcolm fits into the murder, but we can't split up, okay?"

"Do you have a plan?" She scooted in closer to me.

"Wing it? I'm not sure what he knows about the situation or why he left or anything. I'll try to not give anything away. Just back me up, okay?" I had spotted a gift store with a hand-painted sign on the door flipped to OPEN. "Come on, we can start here."

I wrapped Bubbles inside my jacket and zipped up. I wouldn't leave him in the car, but I also didn't want to waltz into a store holding a dog. I pushed open the door, hitting a bell that chimed. The inside was warm, cozy, and stuffed to the gills with items for sale. There was a table full of books: memoirs from religious or noteworthy people, a cookbook of monastery soups, and religious instructions. In fact, a half dozen copies of one of the memoirs I had co-written were stacked between two bookends. I ran my finger across the spines. Something about being surrounded by books made me feel safe and warm, like I was among old friends. The table next to it was a mix of handmade and mass-produced crafts with Bible quotes.

I moved around the room to find some knitted items and picked up a few things: scarves for my mom and sister—all the proceeds went to support inner-city education programs —and a hand-painted cross for Magdalena, who I knew was Catholic. It was a funky mix of colors that I thought she would appreciate.

Bubbles lifted his nose and sniffed the room. It

smelled lightly of an unfamiliar incense or essence. I picked up a candle and deeply inhaled the spicy and masculine scent. I added it to the pile to give to Ryan as a thank-you for introducing me to Prudence. Next to the candles were hand-made lotions with lavender labeled "Bad mood be gone." I barked with laughter and grabbed a tube for Prudence, who I thought might appreciate the humor.

I picked up a little rock with a heart painted on it for Barbie. My arms were starting to overflow with items while I balanced my purse on one arm and Bubbles hid in my jacket.

There was a door ajar behind the counter, and a voice trailed through. "I'm coming. I'm coming."

Through the door popped out a real-life nun in her black-and-white habit. She wore no makeup and had eyes that twinkled. "Hello, girls. Sorry to leave you out here alone, but I was getting myself another cup of tea. It always seems to work that way, doesn't it? No one shows up all afternoon, but the second you leave, visitors show up. Were you here for the morning mass? You're not visitors to our center, are you? Is that a dog? I love animals. May I pet him?"

I felt an instant kinship to this bubbly, smiling lady, but one thing threw me off. How should I address her? The sum total of my experience with nuns and the Catholic Church in general was limited to televisions and movies like *Gone with the Wind* or *Sister Act*. Should I call her Mother? Sister? The bride of Christ?

I pulled Bubbles out of my jacket and placed him on the ground. "He can be a bit skeptical of people, so we'll have to see if he will let you pet him or not, ma'am."

She smiled at me while Bubbles sniffed at her shiny

black shoes. "You can call me Sister Mary." She knelt down, and Bubbles gladly accepted her attention.

"Nice to meet you, Sister Mary. I'm Melissa, that's my friend Rebecca, and this is Bubbles."

Her hand slowed as she petted Bubbles. Then she stood up suddenly and leaned around the counter to examine my face. "You're from the TV show down in Fishcreek Falls. They're saying you might have killed the poor girl." She grabbed my hands and pulled me close to study me.

I shook my head. "No, I didn't kill her."

She nodded and dropped my hands. "I believe you. I have a gift for these things, and whatever sins you have—and we all do—I don't think you killed her."

Rebecca came up next to me. "You watch reality television."

Sister Mary shook her head. "No, but I follow the news closely. You can't service and pray for those in need unless you know who they are. And you and Bubbles have been in the news quite a lot this week." She turned to Rebecca. "Are you on the show as well?"

"I'm the director," she said proudly.

"Wonderful. Women are far too underrepresented in the industry." She turned back to me. "Are you here to get away from it all? Quiet reflection and religious intro-spection?"

"I wish. Actually, a friend from home ran off to join a monastery, and we were able to track him down here. We were hoping to talk to him."

She started to sort through the items I had placed on the counter and began punching amounts into an ancient cash register. "You can't just run off and join a monastery; it doesn't quite work that way. It is a long and drawn-out process so both the church and applicant can make sure it is the right decision, but we do accept people that are temporarily seeking a time of rest. But I can't tell you if your friend is here. That would break a trust that I intend to keep."

I pulled out my wallet and handed her cash. "I understand, Sister Mary, but this is an exceptional circumstance. Please don't repeat this, but I think Malcolm knows something that will clear my name. I didn't kill Stacey, and I want to prove it. As you know, a good name is worth more that silver or gold."

Her eyes had widened slightly at the mention of Malcolm's name. Perhaps she would help me after all, but instead she shook her head. "Proverbs 22 aside, I can't help you in this." She put everything in a bag, handed it to me, and pushed me toward the door. "But maybe God can provide the answers you seek. Over there by the side of the parking lot is an inspiration walk that leads through the woods. Oftentimes I go there to pray, and God reveals His mysteries to me. Go walk and pray. God bless you." She pushed us out the door and slammed it behind us.

I scooped Bubbles into my arms, protecting his delicate feet from the cold Wyoming ground. "Now what? I've prayed plenty about this. Maybe another walk would help but—Look!" I jabbed a finger at the wood sign hand-painted in bright yellow. It said, "Inspiration Walk, a place for quiet reflection. Frog Falls ¼ mile ahead."

Rebecca squeezed my arm. "Could that be the same waterfall from the picture Malcolm sent? Do you think that's what she was trying to tell us?"

I looked over my shoulder to the gift store. No one was in the window, but the curtain on one side twitched mysteriously. "It just might be. Let's find out."

The dirt path ran through a wooded area. Our drive

from Fishcreek Falls had mostly been through wide-open spaces and rolling hillsides of scraggly sagebrush. We had gone over a few passes where the snow was still piled high, but often there were large patches of woods, and the Catholic retreat center was located in one of them. The aspen and pine trees towered overhead, the shadows cold and wet under their boughs.

The path twisted and turned, and quickly the parking lot was lost from sight as the sound of rushing of water increased. We had to hike up a rather steep staircase in the dirt reinforced with wooden planks, and I was panting by the time we reached the clearing, an open area the size of a small bedroom containing a few wooden benches (wood planks across cinder-block feet) facing Frog Falls. On one of the benches, his back to us, was Malcolm, staring at the water.

I took a moment to gather myself. I'd only known him for a short time, but he brought out a whole range of emotions. At first he had been a potential love interest, though that quickly faded to just another in a long line of failed prospects when he'd disappeared. But when I had seen his connection to Mike, he had taken on a sinister appearance. I wasn't sure what to expect from this conversation and took a deep breath to brace myself.

The waterfall was roaring from spring snow melt, and he didn't hear us. I pressed a finger to my lips, and Rebecca nodded and waited for me to make the first move. The waterfall was at least ten feet tall, and the clearing we stood in was at about the halfway point. The top of the waterfall was five feet above the clearing and the pool five feet below the clearing. The edge of the clearing fell straight down to the pool below. The water at the bottom was dark as the sunlight was blocked from the rippled surface.

I handed Bubbles to Rebecca and quietly walked up behind him. "Malcolm."

He jerked around and stood up. "What are you doing here? How did you find me?" He eased back toward the edge of the clearing and pool below. "Did anyone follow you?" He looked at Rebecca over my shoulder and down the path we had walked.

I stepped over the bench and moved into his personal space. "We know."

He took another step back—right off the edge of the clearing, and he fell backward into the pool below. He hit the water back first then flailed and screamed, "Help! I can't swim!"

I ripped off my jacket and shoved it and my purse at Rebecca. I took one stride and jumped out into the air. The fall was only slightly more than that from a diving board, but hitting the water took my breath away. The water was ice cold, and my head instantly ached from the chill. I shivered as water raced into my clothes. Within a few strokes, I had an arm around Malcolm's neck from behind.

"Tell us! What happened?" I screamed above the splashing.

He was fighting me and pulled us both under. He was in a panic when I pushed to the surface, the murky water burning my eyes. I pushed away from him and treaded water.

"No!" His head ducked under, his feet breaking the surface, and I reached out to grab his collar. When his face cleared the water, he screamed, "Mike killed her. I can prove it."

"You promise?"

"Yes, please. I don't want to die."

I shoved him away toward the edge of the pool. "Stand

up." I pushed my feet onto the slick rocks at the bottom of the pool and stood up. It had been deep where we fell in but I had started grazing the bottom of the pool as I struggled with him. The water came to just below my shoulders. He had fallen in backward then flailed around, never realizing that the pool was shallower under where we argued.

"You're going to freeze to death. Get out of there." Rebecca greeted us at the edge of the pool. She jabbed a finger at Malcolm. "Don't think you're getting out of your promise."

Malcolm's blond hair was plastered to his slightly blue face. "No, I want to tell. I haven't slept in a week. Sister Mary told me that I was damaging my soul by holding on to this. Then you showed up. It's a sign."

CHAPTER SIXTEEN

MELISSA

An hour later, I was dry again, and Sister Mary was making Rebecca and me hot chocolate in the cafeteria while we waited for Malcolm. He had gone back to his room to change. I checked my phone for the time.

My hair was still damp, but Sister Mary had helped me buy a dry outfit from the gift store then bagged up my dripping clothing and undergarments. I had on a bright-purple sweatshirt with a front pouch that proclaimed in bold letters that Jesus loved me. I was not embarrassed by the message, which I believed, but by the accompanying cats that decorated the rest of the sweatshirt. I also wore a thick, plaid wool skirt that reached my ankles and a pair of handcrafted leather moccasins from South America. It was a mess of an outfit, but it was warm, and it was unlikely that I would run into anyone I knew.

Malcolm slunk into the cafeteria and sat opposite us. "Hey."

I was unsure how to start the conversation, but Sister Mary joined us and slid three mugs of hot chocolate in front of us. "Go on, Malcolm. Tell them what happened. It'll relieve your burden."

He nodded. The weight of the world seemed to be resting on his rounded shoulders.

Sister Mary placed a plate on the floor in front of Bubbles. "It's boiled chicken. He needs some meat on his bones."

I hadn't brought any food, and it was his dinnertime. "Thank you, for the chicken and the chocolate."

Malcolm let out a sigh. "I've been secretly working for Mike Rickman for a couple of years. I'd get pictures or recordings of people for him to use."

"Blackmail?" I guessed.

He nodded. "He never used those words, but I'm not an idiot. A lot of it was just getting documentation of gossip people already knew or suspected, though sometimes I was surprised. No one was supposed to know that I was working for him, but once or twice, Stacey saw us. I don't know what he told her about that, but he made her stay away from my parents' restaurant. She wasn't super bright, so if he said the food was awful, she just didn't go."

"Did he know about her affair with Carl Beckett?"

Malcolm grimaced. "Yes, he had me get pictures of them together. I can say that was the worst thing I did until this last Monday." He stared at the table.

Rebecca and I exchanged looks. She was smiling, and I elbowed her then jerked my head toward a table set up with coffee urns. "Rebecca, it's going to be a long drive back to town. Why don't you grab some coffee?" She would be able to hear the conversation still, but there was no chance of him catching sight of her excitement.

She stared at me blankly for a few beats before she caught on. "Good idea. I'll leave you two to chat."

Bubbles's toenails clicked as he followed her.

"Malcolm." I waited until he looked up. "What happened on Monday? What happened to Stacey?"

"It started a few months back. Stacey wanted to be on the socialite show, and for once Mike couldn't convince her otherwise. He was worried that being on the show would draw too much attention to her and, through her, to him. So he tried to be sneaky about getting her to quit the show. He sent the pictures I had taken of Stacy and Carl together to Heather, hoping she would be so mad that she'd ditch Stacey, but Heather must have already known, 'cause nothing happened. Then he got the producer not to want her. He figured that was the end of it. But then the episode premiered, and Stacey was all over it." He picked at his fingernails, peeling off a rough corner of skin.

"What happened after the premiere?"

"I saw the show and knew Heather recognized me, but I figured that no one else would catch it. And it wasn't that big a deal." Malcolm's voice rose. "Fishcreek Falls is a small town, and she could have seen me anywhere. Mike was out of town but was coming back first thing in the morning. He called me late Sunday night. He wanted to meet at nine a.m. out in the national forest at a hunting camp that we'd used in the past. Said he could be a couple hours late but to wait for him. He'd pay me five hundred dollars to get there at eight and wait until at least three p.m. It's a solid ninety minutes to get there." He shivered and put his hands around the warm mug.

That had been during the time of Stacey's murder. "You didn't go?"

He sipped the chocolate then nodded. "No. Maybe it was God protecting me or the tone of his voice or that fact that he was cheap and would never offer five hundred bucks for a meeting. I knew something was off but not what. I staked out his house instead. I'm pretty good after all these years. I saw Stacey leave right as Mike got home. She gave him a cheery wave as she passed. He followed her, and I followed him. He didn't even look in his rearview mirror." He shook his head and took another sip.

I knew he didn't want to talk about what had happened next, but I had to keep pushing. "They went to the hotel?"

He nodded. "Stacey went in the front entrance but Mike parked in a different lot, got out binoculars, and watched Stacey. I've done enough stakeouts to know there was a third lot over by the drugstore where I could see both him and the hotel. Stacey went into Carl's office—I saw them through a window—then Mike got out and ran over to the connected restaurant. The second door in Carl's office leads to the restaurant's kitchen, which has a door to the parking lot as well. I saw him slip a gun into his jacket as he jogged. He'd never carried a gun before, so that was unusual. Then I followed Mike. The restaurant isn't open on Mondays, so I wasn't worried about running into any employees. I snuck in very slowly so I wouldn't run into him, and by the time I got to the office door on the far side of the kitchen, Mike and Stacey were already fighting. The door was slightly open, and I got in close."

I leaned over, hanging on his every word. "About?"

"I missed the beginning, but she was saying something about she wanted to live her own life and if he didn't let her, she'd out him. There was some noise, like things being shuffled around. She told him to back up, and he laughed and said something like, 'That's even better.' She yelped then 'bam, bam.' Two gunshots, but they weren't loud. My ears didn't ring or anything. That's when I dropped my recorder."

I was in shock. "You had a recorder?"

"Of course. It's a very small digital recorder but very high end. I was so startled that I dropped it. No lights were on in the kitchen, so I didn't see where it went, but I think it slid then fell through a grate in the floor, like a drain or something. I didn't wait to find out. I got out of there fast. He'd just shot his wife."

"Wow."

"I'm not sure if shooting Stacey was planned, but I'm positive that he was planning to shoot me in the woods that day. There's no cell reception out there, so maybe he planned to go shoot Stacey at the house then me in the woods and frame me. Or make it look like a home invasion at his place and hope that no one ever found my body. Or dump us both out there. I don't know, but..."

"You have to tell the police."

Life shot back into his face. "No! I have no proof. Like I can go to the police and say, 'Hey, I've been helping this guy blackmail people for years, but I swear I'm being honest when I say he shot his wife and I heard it.' I helped him get dirt on some officers and a judge." He buried his face in his hands.

"You need a good lawyer. What if I got you hooked up with the best criminal lawyer in town and brought them out here to talk to you? Would you listen? At least do that, please."

"Really? You'd do that? And not tell anyone where I am?"

Rebecca came over. "I'm really sorry, but we need to go. Ryan just called and is freaking out that we're in Wyoming. They're over at the restaurant now, setting everything up for the filming tomorrow."

Malcolm grabbed her wrist over the table. "Look in the

floor grates near the office down in the kitchen of the restaurant. If you find that recorder, I can give it to my lawyer."

She took his hand off her wrist. "Of course. Anything to help clear Melissa's and your names, okay?"

Sister Mary held open the door. "Please drive carefully, and I'll pray for you."

I smiled at her. "Thank you for everything." I scooped up Bubbles, who was licking his chops in satisfaction, and walked into the parking lot.

As the door closed behind us, I heard Sister Mary ask, "Where did all my coffee go?"

MELISSA

I woke with a start in Rebecca's idling car. It was parked in front of her hotel, and I was alone except for Bubbles asleep in my lap. I checked my phone and gave my sister an update on our location. The second episode of the season had aired, and she wanted to talk to me about how to get Heather off my case and solve the crime.

Then I messaged Maggie to tell her that I had so much to tell her and she should message me ASAP.

Rebecca came out of the front of the hotel carrying a set of keys she shook at me. Leaping into the car, she put it in drive and peeled out. "We have to get out of here before Ryan catches us."

She pulled out of the hotel driveway, but instead of turning left, toward my ranch, she turned right.

"Where are we going?" I asked around a yawn.

"You know how I told you that they set up for filming tomorrow morning? We have a set of keys, so we can go into the restaurant tonight and find that recorder. How awesome is that? Then you can drive back up tomorrow with the recorder and lawyer. This whole case could blow wide open by Tuesday, and we could get your interview into this week's episode. Maybe film some dramatic reenactments. Piece together the extra footage we shot. The network will love it and pick up the show for a full season. We'll be heroes."

"One step at a time," I sighed.

The streets were empty, and all the buildings were dark. It was well past midnight, and I was glad that I could sleep in tomorrow. Bubbles yawned, tucked his head under his leg, and curled into a tight ball.

We pulled into the dark parking lot of the Trumpett Hotel, past the lit but empty lobby, and around to the back door of the restaurant. Rebecca started to unbuckle.

My stomach was queasy, and I hugged Bubbles to my chest. "I don't feel right about this." I didn't want to be here, especially not when I was accused of Stacey's murder. I never wanted to be here again.

"Ten minutes tops. We'll run in. I have keys, and they said I could be here. We'll check the grates, and then I'll take you home. You're looking beat." She hopped out of the car.

I opened my door and called after her, "You're sure a charmer, aren't you?" I followed her to the door as she unlocked it and propped it open a foot. "Aren't we ruining the chain of evidence or whatever?"

"I'm going to film it if we find anything." She stepped into the kitchen of the restaurant and ran a hand over the wall until she flipped on one light. "That's enough. I don't want to turn them all on. Go check the grates. I'll figure out where to stand to film you finding it." She stepped away into the darkness while I searched in the lighted area for a grate.

I walked around the corners, clutching Bubbles to my chest as he contorted his body to sniff everything in the kitchen. Near a door that must have led to Carl's office based on its location, I looked around for a grate. I knelt and looked under a lower shelf. Inset in the tile was a large grate. I dug out my phone and used the flashlight app to see down into the holes. I put Bubbles aside and shoved my head under the shelf, and visible below the grate was a small black, plastic rectangle.

"Stand up slowly and put your hands up. Where's Rebecca?" A man's voice called behind me.

I stood up slowly, and a middle-aged man had a gun pointed at me. I raised my hands over my head. I kept my eyes on his face as Rebecca's shadowy figure ran out the door to the parking lot. "She's not here."

RYAN

Driving through the dark streets, I muttered to myself, "I'm going to kill Bec." She'd taken off the whole day for a side trip. Beth knew I was mad and told me that Rebecca had grabbed the keys to the restaurant at the Trumpett Hotel. I didn't know what she was up to, but sororicide might be the only answer.

I pulled up to the hotel and parked in front. I was halfway to the door when it occurred to me that Bec had the key to the restaurant, which was at the back of the hotel. I jogged around the corner and went cold when I saw Mike Rickman pull a gun from his jacket and duck through the restaurant door. I ran over, and Bec burst out the door. I hugged her to my chest and pulled us back to the wall. "Where's Melissa?"

Bec was sobbing. "Mike has her at gunpoint. He killed Stacey. Malcolm saw it all." She was white and shaking under my grip. I shoved my keys and phone at her. "Go to my car and call the police."

My thoughts narrowed down to one thing now that Bec was safe: Mike was the killer, and he had Melissa.

I slipped through the propped-open door and ducked. The kitchen was a confusion of counters and ovens and stoves. Only one light was on, right above Melissa, who had her hands in the air. Mike's back was to me. He had a gun with a silencer pointed at her.

"No." Her voice shook slightly, but she lifted her chin.

"No? I have a gun. You're coming with me."

I moved in closer on the balls of my feet. Either she didn't see me or she knew better than to look in my direction and give me away.

"I'm not going anywhere with you."

He let out a frustrated growl and swooped down. When he stood, he had Bubbles by the scruff. "I'll kill your dog if you don't get over here."

I moved silently and was almost to the point where I could jump over a countertop to reach Mike from behind when Bubbles twisted and sank his teeth into Mike's hand. He yelped and dropped the tiny dog, who let out a horrible cry as his body hit the tile. Everything moved into slow motion after that.

Mike lowered his gun toward Bubbles and squeezed off a shot as I leaped over the counter separating me from Mike. I was so focused on hitting his arm to remove the gun that I didn't see until the last moment that Melissa was also moving. She plowed her shoulder into his gut. The gun went off, and time sped up again. I slid over the table and onto the hard tile floor on the other side. The impact made my ears ring, or maybe that was the subsequent gunshots. Melissa was a fury of nails, hair, and elbows, her primal scream tearing my ears. I wrestled the gun from his hand, but my right arm wasn't moving correctly. It was dead and heavy.

It could have taken years or seconds, but a new noise was added to the fray. Men yelled, and strong hands pulled me away. An officer had Mike pinned to the floor. "Police! Police! Stop! We've got him."

Melissa had blood all over her face. "Bubbles! My dog." The sheer anguish in her voice tore at my heart. She looked around frantically. I reached out to her, my own hands covered in blood, and drew her around a counter to where I had seen Bubbles land.

Bubbles lay on his side, perfectly still, his eyes staring at nothing. She covered her mouth and kneeled. I could barely hear her speak over the radios, officers yelling, and the approaching sirens. "Oh Lord, please let him be okay."

I was right next to her, my right arm hanging limp at my side, my left arm around her. As she said "okay," he turned his head to look at her. He tried to stand, but yipped and lay back down. She sobbed, and tears poured down her face as she scooped him to her chest.

I looked her over. She did not appear to have been shot, and while I ached all over and seemed to have some flesh wounds, there were no holes in me that I hadn't previously had. I wrapped my one useful arm around them both and held them to my chest.

Someone came over to check us out. "We need to get you to a hospital."

I shook my head. "The dog needs a vet first."

"Ryan! Melissa! You're okay. I'm sorry." Bec ran over and hit my right arm, sending a wave of pain through my body that stole my breath away.

People rushed around, voices disconnected from their owners. "Sir, you need a hospital now. That shoulder's dislocated."

I shook my head and tried to speak, but nothing came out.

An officer loomed into my vision. "Don't worry. We'll take good care of Bubbles. We're big fans." He spoke into the radio at his shoulder. The officer delicately took Bubbles from Melissa's grasp.

I was having problems catching my breath as my world faded to black.

MELISSA

"Melissa, are you sure you're up for this? I'm sure Ryan will understand if you wait until tomorrow."

I looked at my sister aghast. "I can't wait. Last night he saved my life."

Sam sighed. She drove out of the vet parking lot and headed for Ryan's hotel.

I adjusted the baby sling across my chest and checked on Bubbles. The vet had said he was fine; no broken bones or anything, but like me, he was pretty sore and unsettled. The vet had held Bubbles overnight for observation, and I had finally been able to pick him up just now. The employees at the emergency vet had told me about the officer who had raced Bubbles over the night before with sirens blaring and lights flashing. I would need to thank the officer personally, along with everyone else who had helped us.

I settled into the seat and resisted the urge to fall asleep. After the police had arrested Mike, they had rushed Ryan and me to the hospital. Rebecca had ridden with her brother. By the time I could try calling my family, they had already arrived at the hospital.

That was when I found out that Rebecca had live-cast the entire kitchen scene. When Mike had slipped in the door, she had activated the app to show the world that Mike had a gun and was the killer. It was more effective than a phone call to the police. They had already been tailing Mike as the main suspect in his wife's murder.

I had never met Mike before, but I'd guessed who it was when he pulled his gun on me in the kitchen. It might have felt like a lifetime between Rebecca sneaking out, Ryan sliding in, and the police arriving, but the video clocked in at less than three minutes.

Rebecca had told me in the hospital that she had run to call for help, but the police were already pulling into the parking lot. She'd barely had time to tell them that Mike, Ryan, and I were in the kitchen before they ran to save us.

The hospital had cleared me to come home early in the morning. I was banged up pretty good but nothing serious. By the time we'd gotten home, the major news story was the dramatic capture of Mike Rickman. The live feed showed everything starting from the point at which Mike had pulled a gun on me. It included Ryan sneaking up on Mike, Mike dropping Bubbles, Ryan and me disarming him, and the police coming to the rescue. Shortly after the police saved us, Rebecca had ended the video. People were far more upset by Mike hurting Bubbles than they were by him pulling a gun on me. I couldn't blame them; I felt the same.

My parents were waffling between being furious at the risks I'd taken and grateful that I was safe. My sister wanted to know why I was wearing a wool skirt, moccasins, and a purple kitty sweatshirt.

I had fallen into bed and slept until the vet called to say I could pick up Bubbles. It had taken some arm twisting, but I'd convinced Sam to drive me into town. I had texted Ryan to ask if I could stop by, and he had said yes and given me his room number.

Sam pulled into a parking spot at the hotel. "Do you want me to come in?"

"No, I shouldn't be more than a few minutes." I got out of the car and headed in.

When I got to his room, I hesitated before knocking. The adrenaline, lack of sleep, and chaos meant that the seriousness of the situation was still sinking in. I could have been killed the previous night. Ryan had risked his life running into that kitchen to save me and Bubbles. He could have stayed in the parking lot and waited for the police, but he hadn't. I had seen him sneak in the kitchen door, and I knew he would save me. Things had been going well until Mike dropped Bubbles. Though I knew Ryan had a better angle, I couldn't stop myself from attacking Mike. He could have shot me in that moment, but he was too focused on Bubbles.

I was chewing on my lip, reliving the horror of that moment, when Ryan threw open the door. His right arm was in a sling, and he wore a rumpled sweat suit. "Are you just going to stand in the hallway all day?" He walked back into his room and sat at a table.

"How did you know I was out there?" I followed him in and sat opposite him.

"I don't know how someone so delicate and tiny could

be so heavy footed. Clomp, clomp, clomp. My room was shaking. I knew it was you." He gave me a crooked smile and a wink.

I laughed at his teasing and smiled back.

He waved a hand at me to enter, gesturing me to the other chair. "How are you feeling?"

"Better than you."

He shrugged his left shoulder. "Nothing permanent. Are you wearing Bubs like a necklace?"

I reached into the sling to scratch behind Bubbles's ears. "Yes, I am. The vet recommended rest so he can heal up, just to be safe." I fidgeted in my seat. "I'm really sorry that you got hurt. I... I'm just really glad that the police happened to be so close."

He shook his head. "They didn't just happen to be nearby. They were following Mike. He had always been their main suspect, not you, despite what Heather or the newspaper said. They were gathering enough evidence to make sure the charges would stick. The audio they took from us was too muffled to identify the killer on first listen, but they figured they could clean it up, along with other forensics. Plus they already had a good idea that he was blackmailing people. The gun used belonged to Carl. They had figured Stacy pulled it from the bookcase to protect herself and it was taken from her then used. After the episode aired yesterday and you were talking about finding the killer yourself, Mike went over to our hotel to wait. When you and Rebecca got the key, he followed you to the hotel, and the police followed him. They said that I blew right by them on the way to the hotel."

"Wow."

"They would have caught him without your interfering."

"But you wouldn't have it all recorded, would you?"

He narrowed his eyes at me then sighed. "No, but it wasn't worth it."

"Rebecca thought it was," I countered.

"Trust me, she knows exactly how unhappy I am. You both could've... never mind." He leaned back in his seat and winced.

"I owe you, like forever."

He nodded but didn't open his eyes yet.

"I should let you go, but one last question. Are we filming anymore? Did the network pick us up for another season?"

Ryan's eyes opened, and a small smile snuck onto his face. "Rebecca didn't tell you? They called this morning. They made sure to first ask if everyone was okay then immediately launched into business discussions. I had to pass the phone over to Rebecca; the painkillers I'm on are not the best for negotiations. They want to finish a whole eight-episode season. Sure, we don't have much of a crew because a lot of them already booked jobs and I'm in a sling, but we're a go. Ian, our executive producer, flew out this morning. He's taking a break from preproduction on his other show to help us. The network wants all the extra footage we shot at the gun store, with Prudence, and at the Bunny Ear hotel. Turns out Rebecca wasn't waiting in the car for us when we talked to Linda Brown, she was in the hallway recording our audio. She'll have to go back and get Linda to sign a waiver. And she wants to go talk to a Sister Mary?"

I chuckled. "You will like her. She's sassy."

"She's a nun, right?" He lifted one eyebrow.

"Yes."

He shook his head. "I talked to the rest of the cast this morning. Heather is pretty pissed about her restaurant getting shot up but also seemed relieved that Mike was caught. I wouldn't expect an apology from her, but she might be a little bit nicer to you."

"I'd be thrilled if she took it down from raving lunatic to mildly irritated with me. I have a theory on why she was so vocal about me being the killer."

Ryan stretched out his leg and rotated his foot while cringing. "Because she hates you?"

"That's part of it. When I met with Malcolm, he said that he had taken photos of Stacey and Carl together, then Mike sent them to Heather, hoping that Heather would have a fight with Stacey or something. Therefore, Heather knew about the affair. Combine that with Stacey being killed in Carl's office, and she figured her husband was the number-one suspect."

"Makes sense. I'm surprised that she wasn't more mad about the affair. But someone told me that Heather and Carl have an agreement about his affairs."

I could never have imagined living that way. "That's sad, but not sad enough to forget that she got her buddy at the newspaper to write that terrible article."

Ryan chuckled. "They printed a clarification today that it was an op-ed piece. Apparently there's some videos of you going around in which Natasha the reporter is screaming at you? When did you have time to get into a fight with her?"

"I had a very busy Sunday."

"I'd appreciate it if you could have a bit less excitement. We're going to be working together for at least another four weeks, and I might not survive it otherwise." He shook his head.

I really looked at him. His long, lean legs were stretched out, his foot just barely brushing mine. It could have been accidental, but I enjoyed the idea that it was on purpose.

His face was a little paler than normal, but dark smudges under his eyes and the occasional wince crossing his face when he moved made him seem rugged and handsome. I knew I needed to leave, but I wanted nothing more than to stay and just be near him for a bit longer.

I wondered if either of us would survive the rest of filming, but I was excited to find out.

ABOUT NIKKI HAVERSTOCK

Nikki Haverstock is a writer who lives on a cattle ranch high in the Rocky Mountains. She has studied comedy writing at Second City and has published 8 cozy mysteries that are heavy on the humor.

Before fleeing the city, she hosted a competitive archery reality show, traveled the world to study volcanoes, taught archery and computer science at a university and now works on her family's ranch herding cattle. Nikki has more college degrees than she has sense and hopefully one day she will put one to work.

Nikki likes to write comedy pieces that focus on the everyday humor of one-uppers, annoying family members and strange behavior of the ultra-rich. She tried stand up but the cattle weren't impressed.

ALSO BY NIKKI HAVERSTOCK

ACKNOWLEDGMENTS

First and foremost, thank you to my husband John, who encourages and loves me even when I am not very lovable. He also helped me keep Ryan's point of view a bit more manly.

Thank you to Zara Keane, Lydia Rowan, and Sadie Haller. Not only are you all great authors, but you're an endless source of support and information.

To Teresa Johnson, Holly Cooper, Lori Peterson, and Andrea Jane, thank you for the daily messages that keep me from being a total recluse.

Huge, overdue thanks to Brent Trotter and Paris McCoy who kept me sane during my time as a host and executive producer of a competitive reality show. Thank you for teaching me about the business and preventing a complete mental breakdown.

A special thanks to Zoe York. Not only is she a friend, but she hosted an amazing seminar, Romance Your Brand, which focused on building a series. I found the information I learned to be a valuable resource.

Last but not least, thank you to the people that make

this book shine: development editor Jodi Henley, cover artist Rebecca Poole, and Red Adept Editing.

Made in the USA
Las Vegas, NV
25 August 2021